Fall From Grace

Beth Orsoff

Also by Beth Orsoff:

Chapter 1

THEY SAY what doesn't kill you makes you stronger. Bullshit.
What doesn't kill you *almost* kills you. I should know.

"Grace, are you listening?" Dr. Stetler asked.

My head jerked up at the sound of my name, and I found
myself staring into the plain brown eyes of my nemesis. They
were unremarkable in every way, but I'd never forget Dr.
Stetler.

"Yes," I replied before surreptitiously sliding my gaze back
down to my hands, which were absentmindedly picking at the
pilled fuzz clinging to my yoga pants.

Jonah loved my hands. The memory popped into my head
unbidden, as they always did. And as always, the memory made
me smile. Jonah used to tell me I had the hands of a queen,
whatever that meant. I'd asked him, of course. Many times. He'd
always laugh and say it was because my hands were regal. I had
no idea what that meant either, but it became our private joke.
One of many.

My smile faded as I realized that even Jonah wouldn't think
my hands looked regal now. The skin was dry, the fingers bare,
and several of my nails were broken, although I noticed a few of

them were still sporting remnants of the pale pink polish that had been foisted on me a few weeks ago. I'd wanted clear nail polish, but I was overruled. I was also overruled when I said I didn't want a mani-pedi. Operation Get Grace Out Of The House was underway. I had no choice in the matter. I had no choice in lots of things anymore.

"Grace," Dr. Stetler said, pulling me out of my reverie. The man had to be in his late fifties, but he still sported a head of thick salt and pepper hair. "We're all waiting."

I shifted my gaze from Dr. Stetler to the other five faces in our "sharing circle."

The widower in his late sixties who still wept daily for his dead wife and the young mother who had fantasized about drowning her three small children in the bathtub stared at me expectantly. The rest of my unwilling compatriots—an unhappy teenager, a former race car driver who'd lost his leg in a spectacular career-ending crash, and a middle-aged housewife with OCD who had pulled out all her hair and now wore a scarf around her head so she looked like a chemo patient—averted their eyes. I appreciated their disinterest.

I shifted my weight on the unyielding metal folding chair then blurted out, "I'm thinking of changing my name."

"Changing your name to what?" asked Unhappy Teenager.

"You mean go back to your maiden name?" OCD Lady asked. I felt guilty for thinking of her as OCD Lady since I knew her name was Deborah, but that is how I thought of all my fellow patients—not by their names but by the circumstances that had brought them to this place. I assumed they all thought of me as that woman whose husband and baby were gunned down in the street. It was not an entirely accurate portrait of me but close enough.

"Let Grace speak," Dr. Stetler admonished, and both women returned their gaze to the floor.

Did I mention the only thing warm and fuzzy about Dr. Stetler was his flannel shirt?

"No, Deborah." At the sound of my voice, OCD Lady looked up and shot me a tentative smile. "I'm keeping my married name. I'm a widow, not divorced. But I'm thinking of changing my first name to Charlie."

"You can do that?" Unhappy Teenager asked.

"Of course she can," Widower replied. "She can use whatever name she wants."

"Musicians use stage names all the time," Former Race Car Driver opined.

"But isn't Charlie a man's name?" Homicidal Mother asked.

"I think we're getting off track," Dr. Stetler said. "The issue isn't whether Grace can legally change her name, but why she wants to. What do you think changing your name will accomplish, Grace?"

"I didn't say I was changing it *legally*." The law was the one area where I could out expert Dr. Stetler. Of the two of us, I was the only one with a law degree.

"Is that relevant?" he asked. "To your decision, I mean."

As usual, I had no answer to Dr. Stetler's question. Or none I was willing to share with someone I'd met three days ago when I was involuntarily committed to the Wellstone Center, where those who pose a danger to themselves or others and who are lucky enough to have savings or good health insurance, get sent.

By that criteria, I was lucky. The Wellstone Center, with its manicured lawns and sweeping hilltop views, was undoubtedly lightyears better than the psych ward at the county hospital, which was where the unlucky failed suicide attempts were warehoused. God bless America.

Dr. Stetler stared expectantly.

I half shrugged and half sighed in response.

"Is that a yes or a no?" he asked.

3

I took a deep breath before I answered. Unhappy Teenager had already warned me that showing anger was a no-no. "They can use it as an excuse to keep you locked up longer," she'd whispered during the silent walking meditation portion of our mindfulness class. That was why she was now Unhappy Teenager. When she'd arrived at the Wellstone Center three weeks ago she'd been Angry Teenager, she'd confided, "but now I'm just playing their game so I can, like, beat them with their own rules." It seemed like a good strategy.

When I was sure I could keep the irritation out of my voice, I said, "It's relevant to the ease with which it can be done. There are no forms to fill out, no mandatory publication in the newspaper, and no court approval required. I tell people to call me Charlie, and voilà, I'm now Charlie." I folded my arms across my chest and shot him an insincere smile.

"And how will that make you *feel*, Grace?" he asked. "Will you *feel* any different if people call you Charlie?"

My smile faded. It always came back to *feelings* with Dr. Stetler. Didn't he realize it was too many *feelings* that had landed me here? Maybe if I could stop feeling for a while, I could actually survive.

Chapter 2

I'D ONLY BEEN at the Wellstone Center for three days, but I'd already developed a routine. After group session ended, I went back to my room and rested until dinner. But today I didn't have that luxury. My seventy-two-hour involuntary hold was over and my probable cause hearing, which will determine whether I'll be forced to stay at the Wellstone Center for another two weeks or whether I'll be allowed to leave, was set for later this afternoon.

In contrast to the last seventy-two hours, I was suddenly concerned with what I looked like. Justice is supposed to be blind, but any honest lawyer will tell you that's a lie. Appearances matter and I needed to look like a woman embracing life instead of one contemplating death.

I wished I had a suit to wear—no one was going to say I was mentally unstable if I walked into the hearing room looking like a lawyer instead of a patient—but unfortunately, I hadn't packed a bag for this sojourn. After the emergency room transferred me to the Wellstone Center, my aunt dropped off clothes for me but nothing hearing-appropriate. Still, I dug around the small suitcase and under all the yoga pants, sweatshirts, socks, and underwear, I found a pair of purposely-torn designer jeans, a long-sleeve T-shirt, and my old Steve Madden loafers. They would do.

I didn't have access to a hair dryer—it would be easy to strangle oneself with the electrical cord if one were so inclined—so I pulled my in-need-of-a-trim hair into a high ponytail. My aunt hadn't packed any of my makeup, and to be honest, I'd had no desire to wear any before now, so I traipsed down the hall to Unhappy Teenager's room and bartered a Lululemon sweatshirt for mascara, eyeliner, and a lipstick.

Financially, I knew I'd made a bad deal, but it was definitely the right decision. Dr. Stetler confirmed it when I walked into the hearing room, which, to my surprise, was just a conference room with a long oval table (no sharp edges at the Wellstone Center!), surrounded by a dozen soft leather chairs. "Grace, I hardly recognize you," he said.

I couldn't say the same for Dr. Stetler. He was wearing the khaki pants and flannel shirt he'd worn to group session, but over it, he sported a white doctor's coat with his name stitched above the pocket and a stethoscope peeking out the top. I assumed the stethoscope was just for show. When was the last time a psychiatrist had to check a heartbeat?

"Nice to see you too, Dr. Stetler." I gave him my best fake smile. Not for his benefit but to make an impression upon the man seated at the head of the table, who I assumed from the suit and tie he wore and the briefcase open before him, was the hearing officer who would decide my fate.

My patient advocate, a woman named Felicity, who looked young enough to still be under the legal drinking age but who'd assured me that she'd graduated from college two years earlier, motioned for me to take the seat next to her. But before I could reach her, I was accosted by my mother and my aunt.

Felicity had informed me the day before that I had the right to have family members present at the hearing. I figured she was thinking I would want them there for moral support. In actuality, I was thinking if the hearing officer saw I had a family who loved me, it would increase the odds the officer would order my release. Felicity disagreed.

"Sometimes family members want the extended hold granted because they think their loved one would be safer in a treatment facility," she'd said. "No one wants to be the one who asked for their spouse or sibling or child to come home only to have that person attempt suicide again and this time be successful."

"Don't worry," I'd told her. "My family will support me on this."

"How can you be so sure?" she'd asked.

"Because I'm going to tell them if they don't, then I will absolutely, positively find a way to kill myself in here. The *only* way they can keep me safe is to recommend I come home."

"Ummm." Felicity had swallowed hard and glanced around the common room as if she was looking for someone to call for help.

"Joking!" I'd smiled wide, hoping she believed me. I hadn't been joking, but it was clear from her reaction she wasn't onboard with emotional blackmail.

She'd forced a smile. "Right. Good one."

It was my mother's smothering hug that brought me back to the present. Or really the scent of her perfume—Chanel No. 5. It had been her fragrance for as long as I could remember. My dad used to buy her a bottle every year for Valentine's Day. Either she'd stockpiled or she'd started buying them for herself after he died.

"I'm glad to see you're wearing makeup," my mother said as she squeezed me so hard I thought she might break a rib. When she finally released me, she held me at arm's length and examined my face as if she was a jeweler grading a diamond only with stylish red-framed glasses instead of an eye loop. "You need concealer and a good moisturizer. And a brighter lipstick. That color completely washes you out."

I turned away from her before she could see me roll my eyes, although she must've seen my nostrils flare. And there was no way she could've missed my audible deep breath. *Stay calm, no anger, no outbursts.* I could lose my cool *after* I left the Wellstone Center, but not before. Not if I had any hope of going home today.

Aunt Madeline, as always, intervened. She pulled me into a hug of her own and said, "I'll take her for a makeover when she's feeling better, Caroline."

The thought of my aunt, who hadn't even worn makeup to her own wedding, taking me for a makeover, made me smile. Unlike my mother, who had standing appointments with José to dye her mostly gray roots ash blond and Dr. Spangler to administer Botox injections into her laugh lines, Aunt Madeline accepted both her wrinkles and her gray hair with equanimity. Their style and temperament were polar opposites, and their close relationship baffled everyone except them.

I inhaled Aunt Madeline's clean soapy scent, then disengaged myself from her embrace and took the open seat next to Felicity. If this hearing was a numbers game, I'd win. I had four women on my side of the conference table ranging in age from twenty-three year old Felicity to my sixty-two year old mother. Dr. Stetler sat alone. But he had that M.D. at the end of his name, and I feared no matter how well I argued on my behalf, those letters trumped all.

"Is everyone here?" the hearing officer asked. After we all nodded our assent, he snapped his briefcase shut and placed it under the table. "Then let's begin."

Chapter 3

I WAS SURPRISED the process of deciding a person's freedom wasn't more formal. No one had to rise and face a black-robed judge or swear to tell the truth, the whole truth, and nothing but the truth. The hearing officer, who was closer to my mother's age than mine, just turned to Dr. Stetler and asked him to explain why he thought my three-day hold should be extended for another two weeks.

"Grieving is a process," Dr. Stetler began. He spared us all the lecture about the five stages of grief but droned on about my actions, or inactions, since I arrived. In essence, I resisted "sharing," especially in group sessions. I put up walls between myself and others. I seemed unwilling to explore my feelings. I was unenthusiastic about activities. Three days really wasn't enough time to make a suicidal person not suicidal.

It was hard to argue against him since everything he said was true. Luckily for me, I had some training in this area.

"Your honor, sorry, I mean Mr. Rostin." The hearing officer had told us at the outset that he was only an attorney, not a judge, and that the rules of evidence and civil procedure did not apply.

I launched into the speech I'd practiced while lying in bed last night. "First, I want to state at the outset that I'm very sorry for what I did."

"Grace, you don't need to apologize," Felicity interrupted. "You were in pain. You're still in pain. Everyone in this room understands that."

I knew she thought she was helping, but she wasn't. If I was in the same amount of pain now as I was when I tried to kill myself, wouldn't I just try to kill myself again as soon as I left the Wellstone Center? That's the argument I would make if I were sitting on Dr. Stetler's side of the table.

"Thanks, Felicity, but I *do* need to apologize—to my mother. As a parent who has lost a child, I know what that pain is like, and I never should've put my mother through that or even attempted to."

I understood that I couldn't win this case on the facts, so my only hope was to play on the hearing officer's emotions. Not that what I said was untrue. I did feel bad about what I'd put my mother and my aunt, who was like my second mother, through. It's just that at this moment in time their feelings were not my top priority. I was still too mired in my own grief to spend much time worrying about anyone else's.

I took a deep breath and continued. It was much harder saying these words aloud than it had been merely reciting them in my head. "I had two great loves in my life, my husband Jonah and my baby Amelia, and they were both taken from me at the same time." Even saying just that much caused the memory of that day to flood over me and I could feel the tears welling in my eyes. I had no choice but to continue.

"We were having a good morning. Amelia had slept through the night for the first time, which meant Jonah and I had both gotten a whole six hours of uninterrupted sleep. That was cause for celebration in our house. Jonah strapped Amelia into her baby carrier and the two of them hiked down the hill to the bakery for croissants."

I left out the part that Jonah was trying to get back into my good graces after the fight we'd had the night before. I was angry at him because his brother Jake was supposed to drive up from LA to babysit and he'd cancelled on us at the last minute. But those facts didn't help my case.

"I knew I'd have about an hour to myself, a luxury since Amelia was born, and instead of folding laundry or cleaning the kitchen, I decided to treat myself to a bubble bath."

Someone let out a sob, I wasn't sure who. I only knew it came from my side of the table. But I kept my eyes trained on the hearing officer. At this moment, he was the only person in the room whose reaction mattered.

I took another deep breath and continued. "I'd just gotten settled in the tub when the phone rang. I thought about letting it go to voicemail, but I thought it might be Jonah, so I got out and ran to pick it up."

I didn't share with the hearing officer my very clear memory of standing naked next to my bed, dripping water all over the carpet as I listened to a woman with a heavy Indian accent deliver the news that would change my life forever.

Chapter 4

I REACHED for the bottle of water someone, probably Felicity, had placed in front of me and took a sip, trying to steel myself for this next part. "But it wasn't Jonah calling; it was a woman. I don't know if she was a doctor or a nurse or just someone whose job it was to make these kinds of phone calls, but she told me I needed to come to the hospital right away.

At the time I assumed Jonah and Amelia had been hit by a car because people were always taking the curve at the bottom of the hill too fast. It used to make me nervous when I was out walking with Amelia in the stroller. I didn't find out about the shooting until after I arrived."

I grabbed the water bottle, but this time I didn't drink. I just needed something to hold onto. After a long pause I said, "I don't remember a lot of details from the hospital," which wasn't true. I remembered every detail—the smell of antiseptic, the light green walls in the viewing room, the silver gurney with the wobbly wheel. But I knew if I started talking about those details, I'd break down and I couldn't afford to do that. I needed to stay focused on arguing my case.

Yet, I couldn't banish from my mind the image of Amelia's

tiny body on that huge metal table. The hospital worker had tried to get me to identify Amelia's body from a photograph—she said this was the customary procedure now—but I refused. I told the woman I had to see her and hold her and breathe in her baby scent; that was the only way I'd ever believe it was true. Eventually, the woman relented.

Someone had covered the wound on Amelia's head with white gauze, but I learned later that had just been for my benefit. She'd died instantly when the bullet passed through her still-soft skull before it lodged in Jonah's chest. Jonah survived a few minutes longer. His heart stopped in the ambulance. So, all my rushing to get to the hospital quickly—running a red light and almost getting into an accident myself—was for naught. They were both gone by the time I arrived.

I swallowed hard and continued. "In the beginning I slept a lot, or tried to. If I could get myself to fall asleep, even if it was only for a short time, I'd have those first few seconds before I was fully awake when I'd think it was all a bad dream. But eventually even those few seconds of peace disappeared."

I stared up at the hearing officer, whose expression was pained. It was a look I'd seen many times in the last fourteen months. I glanced down at his left hand and noticed the wedding ring, and I wondered if he had any children and if he was imagining what it would be like if what happened to me happened to him. But I didn't ask. I never did.

"So, yes, Mr. Rostin, the night I tried to kill myself I did want to die because I wanted to make the pain go away. I just missed Jonah and Amelia so much that I didn't want to live without them anymore. I didn't see the point of living without them. I knew the only way I would ever get to see them again was to join them—so that's what I decided to do."

"Are you religious, Ms. Hughes?" Mr. Rostin asked.

"No. Not anymore. Not ever really, but especially not now."

Mr. Rostin nodded. That was a feeling most people understood. After a tragedy, some people found solace in religion—my mother, for instance—but others, like me, turned away.

"So it was your grief and your desire to reunite with your family that caused you to attempt suicide. But—" Mr. Rostin glanced down at his notes, "your family was killed over a year ago. Was last week your first suicide attempt? Or were there others before this we don't know about?"

I knew where he was headed with this question, and I needed to put a stop to this line of thinking. "I'm not an impulsive person, Mr. Rostin. I think about things a long time before I act. Suicide's a big decision. I mean, if you do it right the first time you never have to do it again."

Mr. Rostin stared at me open-mouthed. "Sorry, that was a joke. A bad one, obviously. But to answer your question, no, last week was my first attempt." My first *serious* attempt. But I kept that part to myself.

"As my mom and aunt can attest," I turned to them for confirmation, "shortly after... the accident I joined a support group, and at the suggestion of one of the other participants, I became a gun control advocate. I thought maybe if I could help get legislation passed, Jonah's and Amelia's deaths wouldn't be in vain. Maybe something good could come out of this and it wouldn't all feel so pointless."

"It was after the legislation failed," Aunt Madeline chimed in, "that we really saw the change in Grace. It was as if she'd channeled all her grief into her advocacy work. It anchored her to the world, and without that outlet, she started to spiral downward."

"I think the only time she ever ate in the last month was when one of us came over and forced her to," my mom added. "The same for bathing and leaving the house. It's as if she just gave up."

I nodded because it was true. "And that's when..." I didn't need to fill in the rest. They all knew the details—the pills, me unconscious on the bathroom floor, the trip to the emergency room. But none of them knew what had really prompted my suicide attempt that night, and I wanted to keep it that way—both for his sake and for mine.

Chapter 5

"AND NOW, Ms. HUGHES?" Mr. Rostin asked. "Do you feel like you're a danger to yourself or others? Do you think if I send you home today you might try this again?"

"No," I replied. I opened my mouth to launch into my closing argument when Dr. Stetler interrupted. "I'm sorry, Grace, but I disagree."

I wanted to reach across the table and strangle him, but I restrained myself.

"From everything Grace has told us," Dr. Stetler continued without waiting for Mr. Rostin to ask for his opinion, "it appears she feels exactly the same way today as she did when she arrived three days ago. Nothing's changed."

"Everything's changed," I cried.

"In what way?" Mr. Rostin asked.

I'd prepared for this question. "Well, for one thing I realized that even if I had been successful, I still wouldn't be with Jonah and Amelia. Suicide is a sin."

My mother patted my hand. "The church a lot more understanding about suicide now than they used to be."

That was news to me. "Suicide's not a sin anymore?"

Because I definitely remembered the nuns telling us that suicide was a sin when I went to Catholic school.

"No," my mother replied, "it's still a sin. But you can ask God for forgiveness."

"God took my baby, Mother. I'm not asking God for forgiveness for anything!"

She shook her head and sighed, and I turned back to Mr. Rostin. "So, besides the whole not getting into heaven thing, I just realized it was stupid and not something I'm planning on trying again."

Mr. Rostin nodded. "What are your plans for when you leave here?"

I had anticipated this question too; I just hadn't come up with a good answer. I had absolutely no idea what I was going to do when I left the Wellstone Center. At this moment, all I wanted was to go back to my house, lie down on the couch with my favorite blanket, and never leave again. But I knew that answer would get me another two weeks of involuntary commitment, so I gave him the best response I could say with a straight face. "I can't imagine I'll ever make peace with what happened, but I have to find a way to live with it, to move on with my life. I'm still working on the specifics of what that looks like."

"That's something I can help with, Grace."

Ugh. Dr. Stetler again. When he kept his mouth shut, I could almost forget he was in the room.

"It doesn't have to be involuntary commitment," Dr. Stetler continued. "You can check yourself into the Center voluntarily, and you can choose to leave whenever you want."

"I want to leave now. I hate it here." I almost said, "and I hate you too," but I stopped myself in time.

Dr. Stetler sighed. "The Wellstone Center is an excellent facility, but it's not the only one. My point is you haven't dealt with your grief and you need to, and it's not something you should try to do alone. I'd—"

"Grace won't be alone," my mother said. "When she leaves here, she'll be living with me."

I was as surprised by this statement as Dr. Stetler.

I turned to my mom. "Excuse me?"

"Your aunt and I talked about it last night. We agree with Dr. Stetler that you shouldn't be living alone right now. It's not good for you."

"Mom, this is not what we discussed!" She'd agreed to support my decision to leave the Wellstone Center, and that's why I'd asked her to come to the hearing today. She'd never even hinted at me moving in with her.

"We didn't discuss it," my mother said. "You lectured. And I will not be blackmailed."

"Blackmailed?" Mr. Rostin's eyebrows shot up so high they nearly disappeared into the lines on his forehead.

My mother was not helping my case! I should've listened to Felicity. I smiled at Mr. Rostin. "Not blackmailed. Persuaded."

"Yes," my mother said, "Grace persuaded me that the Wellstone Center is not an environment in which she can heal. She needs to be out in the world with other people, not locked away in an institution or holed up in her house."

"I like my house!"

"It's not a house, it's a mausoleum! A shrine to Jonah and Amelia. You need to sell it and move some place new. Some place with less memories."

"You think that's the solution? That if I throw away all their stuff and move to a new neighborhood, I'll suddenly forget about them and be happy again?"

"Not forget, Grace," Aunt Madeline said. "No one is suggesting that. We just don't think it's good for you to wallow in the memories. No one here is going to force you to sell your house or throw anything away." My mother attempted to interject, but Aunt Madeline cut her off. "You just need to leave it all behind for a little while so you can heal."

"And where am I supposed to do all this *healing*?" I asked.

"I thought you could move in with me," my mother said.

"Where would I sleep, Mom? You sold the house right after Daddy died."

"Because I took my own advice," my mother said, her angry tone matching mine. "I didn't need to be rambling around in that big house all by myself. I've made a lot of friends where I'm at now. I keep very busy."

That was true. After my dad died, my mom moved into a fifty-five and over community and now she was constantly on the go—yoga classes, bridge tournaments, pickleball matches. It was like summer camp for senior citizens. But I was too young to live in her condominium even if I wanted to, which I didn't.

"I checked the community bylaws last night," my mother continued, "and it says I'm allowed to have guests under fifty-five stay with me for up to six months."

"And after that?" I asked. "You kick me out onto the street?"

"Don't be ridiculous, Grace. I would ask for a waiver and if they wouldn't give me one, I would move. But I assumed by then you'd want your own place."

Good assumption since I wanted my own place now.

"Or," my aunt said, "you could just move in with me."

Chapter 6

"LIVE WITH YOU?" my mom and I asked simultaneously.

"Yes," my aunt replied. "Live with me."

"At the Guest House?" I asked.

It wasn't really a guest house, that's just what we all called it. In reality, it was a formerly dilapidated, four-bedroom Craftsman in downtown Santa Veneta, which my aunt had purchased for a pittance before the real estate market rebounded and the gentrification of the downtown area began. At the time we all thought she was crazy, but that was before everyone started eschewing hotels for rentals on VRBO and Airbnb.

"Yes," my aunt replied.

"You want Grace to live in a hotel?" my mother asked.

My mother had never been onboard with my aunt's plan to spend her second career ("I'm too young to retire!" my aunt had insisted) teaching at a local community college and converting her house into a B&B. But Aunt Maddy told us that after thirty years as a journalist stationed in hot spots ranging from Mexico City to the Middle East, she was ready to set down roots. My mom and I both thought that after Uncle Ben was killed in Syria (right after capturing the photo that won him a posthumous Pulitzer), Aunt Maddy just wanted to come back to the United States where she felt safe. The irony of Jonah's and Amelia's shooting death in the supposedly safe American suburbs was not lost on any of us.

I think what my mother was really upset about was that Aunt Maddy hadn't chosen to set down those roots in San Francisco. But my aunt always said the reason she could maintain a close relationship with my mother despite their many differences was because they were separated by entire continents. That wasn't true anymore—Santa Veneta was only a five-hour drive or a one-hour plane ride away from San Francisco. But even that relatively short distance gave us both some breathing room from my mother, whose intentions were usually good but whose implementation was often faulty.

"It's a bed and breakfast, Caroline, not a drug den."

"Yes," my mother said, "but you still have strangers coming and going all the time."

"Why would that be a problem?" I asked. "Aren't you the one who's always telling me I need to get out more and meet new people? And we all know you really mean single men."

"Well, it wouldn't be the end of the world for you to go on a date," my mother replied. "You're a young woman, Grace. You can start over. You *should* start over."

I dropped my head into my hands. "Oh my god, I think I really am going to lose my mind."

My aunt pushed away from the table and inserted herself between my mother and me. "No one's losing their mind on my watch. Got it?"

"Got it," I replied, although I wasn't so sure.

She turned to my mother. "Zip it, Caroline. Grace has enough to deal with right now."

"Zip it? I have a right to tell my own daughter what I think,

Maddy. She's *my* child, not yours. If you want to play parent, you should've settled down sooner and had one of your own."

"Ladies," Mr. Rostin called out before Aunt Madeline could reply. "I think that's a conversation for another time and place, don't you?"

Aunt Maddy glared at my mother but returned to her seat.

"I believe I've heard enough to make my determination," Mr. Rostin continued. Then he directed his attention to me. "Grace, you've been through a terrible experience, and I won't pretend to understand the depths of your grief. But my responsibility here today is to decide whether you are a danger to yourself or others. If I find you are, I have no choice but to extend your commitment. If I find you're not, you're free to leave. This is never an easy decision."

Uh-oh.

"I agree with Dr. Stetler that you've not really dealt with your loss, and I think you would benefit a great deal from grief counseling. You're obviously an intelligent woman—"

"Thank you," I said.

"Don't thank me yet."

Double uh-oh.

"But the problem when dealing with intelligent people in these circumstances is that they know, or think they know, the answers I want to hear. Instead of being truthful—"

"I've been truthful." Mostly.

"I believe you have," Mr. Rostin said. "But we both know even truthful statements can be shaded to one's advantage. In any event, Ms. Hughes, I think you need help. And I don't consider that a sign of weakness but a sign of your humanity."

I made the mistake of glancing over at Dr. Stetler, who wasn't even trying to hide the smug expression on his face.

"However," Mr. Rostin continued, "that doesn't mean you need to get that help here."

"I can provide a list of other facilities that can take over Grace's care," Dr. Stetler said.

"That won't be necessary," Mr. Rostin replied, then turned his attention back to me. "Are you willing to live with either your mother or your aunt, at least on a temporary basis, and agree to meet regularly with a grief counselor outside of this facility?"

"Yes. Absolutely."

"If you can commit to that, and I'm going to keep tabs on you to make sure that you do, then I see no reason to extend your hold."

"So I'm free to leave?" I asked.

"Yes, Ms. Hughes, under those conditions you're free to leave."

"Yes!" I fist pumped the air. Dr. Stetler's heavy sigh merely increased my glee. Not only had I won back my freedom, but I beat my nemesis too!

I hugged Felicity first, then my mother and my aunt. Then I thanked Mr. Rostin.

"I wish you the best of luck, Ms. Hughes," he said, placing his pad and pen back in his briefcase. "And if I may, I'd like to offer you a piece of advice."

"Of course." At that moment I wouldn't have refused Mr. Rostin anything.

"Don't hide from the grief. I know it's tempting to bury yourself in work or some other project so you don't have to think about all that you've lost, but that's a short-term solution. In the long run, you need to feel the pain in order to move on."

I heard his words, but I wasn't really listening. At that moment all I could think of was the scene from the movie *Braveheart* when Mel Gibson's character shouts, "Freedom!" I felt that same exultation.

It didn't occur to me until much later that within seconds of

Mel Gibson exclaiming "Freedom!" the bad guys chopped off his head.

Chapter 7

"We're just stopping at your house long enough for you to pick up some clean clothes," my mother said. "Then we're going to your aunt's."

I didn't respond. Instead, I continued to stare out the car window from the backseat. The sun was low in the sky, and although the spring foliage was in full bloom, there was still a slight chill in the air. The joggers, dog walkers, and moms, dads, and nannies pushing strollers through the neighborhood were all still dressed for winter, which in Southern California meant fleece sweatshirts and puffer jackets.

My mother continued to drone on, directing most of her monologue to my aunt, who was driving, while I continued to daydream. Since Jonah's and Amelia's death, I'd begun thinking of my life in two parts—there was Before and there was After. Since the dawn of After, my preferred way to spend my time was to daydream about Before.

"Where should we go for dinner?" my mother asked, interrupting one of my favorite memories of Amelia, the one where we babbled back and forth as if we were having an actual conversation. "I know there's that Italian place you like. We could go there. Or the Greek place. Or one of those restaurants down by the water if you don't mind the drive. Anywhere really, except Mexican."

My mother was the only California native I knew who didn't like Mexican food. Actually, she was the only person I knew from anywhere who didn't like Mexican food. "I'm not hungry," I said without thinking, and immediately regretted it.

"Grace, you need to eat. You're skin and bones. We never would've agreed to take you home if we knew you were going to stop eating again. You promised the judge—"

"He wasn't a judge, Mom, just an attorney, like me."

"I don't care if he's the King of England, you need to eat!"

I stopped listening and returned my thoughts to Before, Jonah this time. Would he think I was too thin? According to my weigh-in at the Wellstone Center, I was down to my high school weight. I had the figure of a high schooler too. All that jiggly flesh on my ass and thighs had disappeared, along with my breasts. Yes, Jonah would think I was too thin. He liked a woman with curves.

I smiled to myself recalling how frustrated I'd been trying to lose the baby weight after Amelia was born. No matter how many kale salads I ate or how many miles a day I walked with Amelia in her stroller, those last five pounds stubbornly refused to leave my body. But that was Before. After, those five pounds melted away, along with many more. As anyone who's ever experienced it can tell you, the Grief Diet is foolproof.

"Grace, are you listening?" my mother asked.

"Yes," I lied.

"So you're okay with seafood?"

"Sure," I said, then leaned my head against the window and closed my eyes.

. . .

SINCE THE RESTAURANT was closer to the freeway, we ate dinner first and drove to my house afterward. Being home again was much harder than I thought it would be. My house had always been my refuge from the world, especially after Jonah and Amelia died. But now it was the scene of my crime.

When I walked into the master bedroom, my stomach seized and I thought I might vomit up the few shrimp I'd managed to force down at the restaurant. I ran into the bathroom and lifted up the toilet seat, which was always down now that I lived alone, but nothing came up. When I returned to the bedroom, I found my mom and my aunt making the bed.

"Stop!" I yelled.

"We're just straightening up," my mother said, smoothing out the wrinkles in the duvet.

"No!" I grabbed the corner of the blanket and yanked it onto the floor. "I need to change the sheets. And the covers. Actually, I want a whole new bed." I tried pushing the mattress off its platform, but it didn't budge. "Can one of you help me, please? This thing is heavy."

My mom and aunt exchanged a look. "Whatever you want, Grace," my aunt said and placed her hand on my shoulder. "But it's late. Why don't we leave it for tonight? We'll come back in the morning."

"It can't wait until morning," I said, ripping at the sheet, which was fitted and tucked tightly under the heavy latex mattress. I threw myself onto the floor and tried to push up the corner of the mattress with one hand while unhooking the sheet with the other. I knew I was acting crazy, but I didn't care. This bed was a crime scene and I had to destroy the evidence.

My aunt knelt down next to me and reached for my hand. "Grace, stop."

"I can't stop," I said, the tears now streaming down my cheeks, whether out of guilt or grief or frustration, I couldn't say.

Maybe a combination of all three. "You don't understand. You don't know what happened."

"We know what happened," my mother said, "and we forgive you. Now you need to forgive yourself."

But she didn't know. No one did. Well, one other person knew, but he wasn't talking. I wondered if he felt as guilty as I did.

Chapter 8

AFTER STRIPPING THE BED, vacuuming the mattress on the strongest setting, and leaving all the bedroom windows open despite the chilly night air, I packed a bag and my aunt drove us back to the Guest House. It was still early in the season and the couple staying in the Ocean Room, so named for its view of the Pacific if you leaned your cheek against the window and squinted, had checked out the day before my suicide attempt, conveniently leaving it free for my mother.

I dropped my bag in the Starfish Room at the opposite end of the hall. It was the smallest room in the house and, according to my aunt, the one that was booked least often, which was a plus for me since I already felt guilty about her losing potential income due to my extended stay. The room's only furniture was a double bed, a dresser, and a nightstand. In that respect, it was not unlike my room at the Wellstone Center, except that the wall behind the headboard was painted a deep aquamarine blue and the windows actually opened and were not made of shatter-proof glass.

I had just started unpacking my suitcase when my mother

appeared in the doorway. "I planned to fly home tomorrow. But I can cancel my flight and stay if you want."

I knew she wanted me to ask her to stay, but I couldn't bring myself to do it. It would be hard enough living here with my aunt watching my every move, I couldn't deal with my mother too. "No, I'm fine."

Although we were the only two guests on the floor, she still shut the door behind her and lowered her voice. "Grace, you're not fine. You just tried to kill yourself."

"I know, Mom. I haven't forgotten."

"And what was all that fuss about the bed? When I suggest you do a little redecorating you bite my head off, but now you want to throw out a perfectly good mattress?"

That topic was not open for discussion. "I'm taking your advice. I thought you'd be happy."

"My advice was to get rid of the baby furniture and turn the nursery back into a guest room. And you should donate all of Amelia's clothes and toys while you're at it."

The tears erupted, as they always did when we talked about Amelia. Not heaving sobs this time; just rivulets of water that quietly slid down my cheeks.

"Oh, Grace." My mother enveloped me in a Chanel No. 5-scented hug. "I don't know what to do for you anymore. Maybe taking you home was a mistake."

I pulled away from her and wiped my eyes. "No. Taking me home was the right thing to do. I mean, I know I have problems, but I'm not going to solve them in an institution."

"Then what's the plan, Grace? You need a plan. You can't continue this way. You're killing yourself. Literally. Even before you took the pills."

I sat down on the edge of the bed and dropped my head in my hands. "There is no plan, Mom. I have no idea what to do."

I used to have plans. Lots of them. I never understood

people who *didn't* make plans. How were you going to get somewhere if you had no idea where you were going? It baffled me. Sure there were variables, the details might change, but you had to know your destination if you had any hope of finding it.

Even before I met Jonah, I had a life plan. I would get married and have kids, but first I would build my career. When I met Jonah during my second year of law school, he fit neatly into my plans. He'd just started an MBA program and wanted a family too but not right away. Our life plans synched up perfectly.

We waited until after we both graduated before we got engaged, and we didn't even consider starting a family until a few years after we were married. That was when we'd first talked about leaving Los Angeles. Although we enjoyed our child-free life in LA, between the cost of housing and the cost of private school, the idea of raising children in the city was daunting. Then Jonah was offered a job at a financial management firm in Santa Veneta, a small city an hour and a half's drive (or two and a half hours in traffic) north of Los Angeles.

My aunt had moved to Santa Veneta a couple of years earlier so we knew the area. It was a less urban than Los Angeles, but it had a handful of good restaurants and a nice beach. Its biggest selling point was that you could still buy a decent house in a neighborhood with good public schools for the cost of a two-bedroom condo in LA.

When Jonah received the job offer, I thought it was fate; a sign that it was meant to be. I immediately started sending my résumé to Santa Veneta law firms, and six weeks later Jonah and I were packing our clothes and books into boxes and selling off our mismatched furniture. Our location was changing, but the plan was the same.

I got pregnant with Amelia the month after we moved into our house. That created new variables: Continue to work full-time or try to cut down to part-time? Hire a nanny or look for quality daycare? Try to get pregnant again soon so our kids would be close in age or wait a few years to give ourselves a break?

Before I could tell you about the trips we'd take to Disneyland when the kids were young and Europe when they were older and could appreciate the culture. I was going to be the parent who volunteered for school field trips, and Jonah would be the parent who coached our kids' sports teams. But we'd still go on date nights once a month to keep our love alive.

But that was all Before.

Now I lived in After, and I didn't see the point of plans anymore. I barely saw the point in continuing to breathe.

My mother sat down next to me and reached for my hand. "Promise me tomorrow you will call a therapist and make an appointment."

"I don't know any therapists, Mom." That wasn't true. I knew several, just none I wanted to talk to.

"Grace, you promised the hearing officer you'd go to grief counseling. That was one of the conditions for us taking you home. If we can't trust you—"

"Fine, I'll call Felicity tomorrow for some recommendations."

And just like that I had a plan.

Chapter 9

"GRACE, I was just about to call you!" Felicity said.

I was surprised she'd picked up. I didn't think anyone under twenty-five actually answered their phone anymore. I thought they all just texted. "You were?"

"Yes, I wanted to check in and see how you were doing. The first night home can be rough. I was waiting to call because I didn't want to wake you."

No danger of that. After Jonah and Amelia died, my doctor gave me a prescription for sleeping pills. But I'd used them all on my suicide attempt, and no one at the Wellstone Center would give me any more.

"I'm an early riser these days."

"That's so great," she said. "I try to hit the gym before work most days, but you know how that goes."

"Yes." Or I used to. I hadn't been back to my old law firm since before Amelia was born. I was scheduled to return to work two days after she'd died, but I ended up spending that morning at the funeral home instead.

"My friend keeps telling me about this great sunrise yoga

class on the beach. I've never been, but her Instagram pictures are amazing. You should check it out."

"Yeah, maybe." I couldn't think of anything I'd rather do less. "So the reason I'm calling is I was wondering if you could give me the name of a grief therapist. I know I could call Dr. Stetler but—"

"Don't. He'll just send you to someone as arrogant as he is."

I laughed, glad she saw through his saintly doctor routine too.

"Sorry," she continued. "I shouldn't have said that. Please don't tell anyone. I don't want to get fired."

"Who would I tell? Besides, you think anyone would listen to the crazy lady who tried to off herself?"

"You're not crazy! You're just suicidally depressed."

Was that better? Obviously, Felicity thought so. "Thanks. I think. So, about that referral?"

I heard the screech of brakes and a horn honking, so I knew she was in the car. "I know the perfect person. I'll text you her info. Some people find her too brusque, but I think you two will get along great."

I was in luck, according to Dr. Helen Rubenstein. Her usual one o'clock appointment had cancelled so she could see me that afternoon. I wasn't sure I was ready to see her that soon—I'd been thinking a few days from now or maybe next week—but she'd returned my call while I was eating breakfast (or my mom and my aunt were eating breakfast while I was nibbling on a slice of toast wishing my aunt had a dog that I could surreptitiously feed under the table like I used to with my dog when I was a kid), and my mom and aunt both insisted I grab the appointment.

"I thought you wanted me to take you to the airport," I whispered to my mom while I held my hand over the phone's microphone.

"Your aunt can take me," she replied.

I turned to Aunt Maddie. "I thought you had a dentist appointment today and that's why I had to drive."

"I'll reschedule," my aunt said and jumped up from the table, leaving her scrambled egg whites behind.

That's how I knew she was lying. Aunt Maddie always cleaned her plate. "You don't really have a dentist appointment, do you? You're just trying to get me out of the house."

Aunt Maddie turned on the kitchen faucet full blast so she could claim not to hear me, but I wasn't fooled. I was about to call her out when my mother placed her hand on mine, forcing my attention back to her. "Don't blame Maddie. It was my idea."

That I believed. "Mom, you need to stop."

"I'm your mother, sweetheart. I'm never going to stop worrying about you."

"Can't you worry without interfering?"

"No," my mother said and took another sip of her coffee.

I believed that too.

My mom and aunt dropped me off in front of Dr. Rubenstein's office building on their way to the airport. They wanted to park the car and walk me inside too, but I forbade it. Just because I'd attempted suicide didn't mean I was an invalid. I was perfectly capable of walking across an atrium and up one flight of stairs by myself.

Dr. Rubenstein was one of five names listed on the door to the suite and there was no receptionist, only a sign notifying patients that they should push the button next to their doctor's name on the panel and have a seat. The waiting room was empty except for me so I had my choice of magazines. I had only been flipping through the latest issue of *People* for a few minutes when an older woman wearing a navy pantsuit and four-inch heels appeared in the doorway.

"Grace?"

"Yes?"

She held her hand out to me. "Hi, I'm Helen Rubenstein."

I wasn't sure what I was expecting a grief counselor to look like, but whatever it was, Helen Rubenstein wasn't it. Maybe because Felicity had recommended her, I'd assumed she'd be younger. And more of a free-spirited type. Someone in a peasant skirt wearing long, dangly earrings. Definitely not the woman standing before me, with her silver hair cut into a stylish bob and wearing a statement necklace, who I would've guessed spent her days barking orders at subordinates from her corner office.

Helen led me down the hall to her suite, which contained a large wooden desk, an Eames-style chair and ottoman, and a tufted green sofa similar to the one I wanted to buy when Jonah and I moved into our house, before he convinced me to purchase the more practical brown leather sectional instead. It was obvious even before she sat down that the chair and ottoman were for Dr. Rubenstein, so I settled into the corner of the couch.

"What brings you here today, Grace?"

"You mean besides the suicide attempt?" I'd told her that much on the phone.

She smiled. "Do you always use humor to deflect from questions that make you uncomfortable?"

Wow, Felicity wasn't kidding. Touchy feely Dr. Rubenstein was not.

"In my experience," Dr. Rubenstein continued, "people

attempt suicide for a handful of reasons, but by far, the most common is depression. Are you depressed, Grace?"

I thought back to Felicity's description of me—not crazy, only suicidally depressed! "Probably."

"I'll take that as a yes. Do you know *why* you're depressed?"

Finally, a question I could answer. I gave Dr. Rubenstein the thumbnail version of Jonah's and Amelia's murders. She nodded empathetically, asked a few follow-up questions, and handed me a box of tissues when the tears inevitably came.

I was just starting to get comfortable talking to her when she said, "I want to thank you for sharing that with me, Grace. I know it must've been painful for you. But now I'd like you to tell me the real reason you tried to kill yourself."

"My husband and child were gunned down on the street. Isn't that reason enough?"

"I'm sorry, I'm not being clear. I apologize. What I meant was, until recently you had been dealing with your grief."

"Not well, apparently. At least not according to my mom and my aunt."

Dr. Rubenstein gave me a genuine smile. "Family members can be well meaning, but they often want their loved ones to grieve in a certain way or on a specific timeline. But there is no right way to grieve; no set schedule everyone follows. And it's often two steps forward and one step back. Give yourself permission to grieve in whatever way you need to, okay?"

"As long as I don't try to off myself again?"

"Suicide isn't grieving, Grace, it's giving up. Although sometimes it can be a call for help. Is that what it was for you?"

I thought back to that night. "No, at that moment I wanted to die."

"And why did you want to die, Grace? Why, *in that moment*, did it seem like the right choice, maybe the only choice?"

"I don't know," I lied. "I was just so sad. And I missed them so much. I guess I just didn't see the point of living anymore."

"Is that all?"

"Isn't that enough?"

Dr. Rubenstein sighed. "Grace, I want to help you. And I think you're here because you want help. Just coming to see me today was a great first step. But the only way I can truly help you is if you're honest with me."

"I am being honest!"

She placed her pen and pad on the desk behind her and leaned forward in her chair. "You've been dealt a shitty hand, Grace. You have every right to feel depressed. Suicidal feelings in these circumstances are not uncommon. But when someone acts on those feelings, it's often because they've been triggered by an event. It could be anything, something that in hindsight seems trivial, but in that moment seemed insurmountable. Or maybe it's something you don't want to admit, not even to yourself."

I wondered if Dr. Rubenstein had ever worked in law enforcement. Jonah's brother used to regale us with tales of how he and his colleagues would get suspects to confess. But I'd kept my secret the whole time I was at the Wellstone Center, and I didn't intend to start blabbing now.

"No, nothing."

"Grace, I've been doing this for over thirty years. I've worked with all kinds of people from all walks of life. There is absolutely nothing you could tell me that would shock me. Nothing I haven't heard some version of before."

I pressed my lips together and stared down at the industrial brown carpet. I really wished I'd worn a watch. Pulling my phone out of my purse to see how much time we had left seemed rude.

"You know everything you tell me is confidential. Legally, I'm not allowed to share it with anyone without your consent."

That wasn't entirely true. Psychologists could disclose patient information in limited circumstances. But I didn't think I fit within the exception to the rule. At this point, I wasn't a danger to myself, and I'd never been a danger to anyone else.

"Grace, no matter what you say to me, I won't judge you. I'm not the morality police. Whatever you're thinking, whatever you're feeling, whatever you did or didn't do, it can be forgiven. No one is irredeemable. Only death is irreversible. Everything else can be fixed."

That's when the tears started flowing.

And the words soon followed.

Chapter 10

"JONAH HAS A BROTHER," I said, when I finally stopped sobbing. "Jake. Or Jacob but everyone calls him Jake."

"Older or younger?" Dr. Rubenstein asked as she passed me a fresh box of tissues.

"Older, by three minutes. They're twins. They were twins."

Dr. Rubenstein nodded. "Fraternal or identical?"

"Identical."

"Do you still see him since Jonah's death?"

"Sometimes."

"That must be hard for you, to see someone alive and well who looks so much like Jonah."

"Yes."

"When you see Jake, does it make you think about Jonah?"

"Yes."

"And when you're with Jake, do you ever feel like you're with Jonah?"

I swallowed hard, uncrossed and re-crossed my legs, and plucked a fresh tissue from the box. But when I glanced over at Dr. Rubenstein she was sitting still and staring at me. "Sometimes," I finally said.

She paused before she asked her next question. "Have you ever imagined that Jake was Jonah?"

I couldn't force myself to say the words, so I just nodded.

Dr. Rubenstein nodded too. "And have you and Jake ever... been intimate?"

The sob shot out of me like a primal scream, followed by "I'm sorry."

Dr. Rubenstein moved from her chair to her ottoman. She was sitting so close to me that she could reach out and touch me, which, to my immense surprise, is what she did next. I didn't think touching was allowed in therapy, but that didn't stop Dr. Rubenstein from grabbing my hands as she said, "Listen to me, Grace. You have nothing, absolutely nothing to be sorry for. You didn't do anything wrong."

I shook my head. "I did. I cheated on Jonah. I cheated on my husband with his twin brother." The pain from saying the words aloud was intense. My heart felt like it was being squeezed in a vise. "What kind of a person does that?" I asked, but I already knew the answer. A horrible one, that's who.

"You slept with Jake before or after Jonah's death?"

"After! I never cheated on Jonah when he was alive. I never even thought about it. I loved my husband."

"I'm sure you did, Grace, and that you still do. But being intimate with someone after your spouse dies isn't cheating. Don't you think Jonah would want you to find love again?"

"Not with his twin brother!" The two were always very competitive.

"And do you love Jake?"

"No! I mean, not in that way. We didn't even..." The memory of that night flooded over me.

"Have intercourse?" she asked.

I shook my head. "Almost. But then I realized it wasn't Jonah and I stopped."

"And you thought it was Jonah when you started?"

"I don't know." It was all so confusing. Some parts of that night were a blur, but other memories played in my mind over and over again in an endless loop. "He was in town for work—"

"Jake doesn't live here?"

I shook my head. "He lives in LA. But he used to come up to visit. He and Jonah were really close. They would shoot hoops together or go surfing or just sit around the house drinking beer and watching a game on TV." I smiled thinking back to the time the three of us went to the beach together. I'd just found out I was pregnant and I had all-day morning sickness. I spent the entire time sitting under an umbrella trying not to puke. "Jake still visits sometimes if he's in town for work. Or at least he says he's in town for work."

"You don't believe him?"

"I don't *not* believe him. It's just that sometimes I feel like he's checking up on me. Other times I think he's lonely. With Jonah gone I'm his only family. Their mom died a few months after Jonah and I got married and their dad was never around, not even when they were kids."

"And the incident you're referring to. Jake came to visit you?"

"Yes. He wanted to go out to dinner but I didn't want to leave the house, so he cooked for me instead. My mom probably put him up to it. At that point everyone was trying to get me to eat."

Dr. Rubenstein smiled. "You are very thin."

"Grief diet."

Dr. Rubenstein nodded. I didn't need to explain.

"So Jake cooked some pasta because that's all I would eat and he opened a bottle of wine. I don't remember drinking that much, but I didn't eat much either and I guess the alcohol went to my head. At first it was wonderful. It felt like I was having dinner with Jonah again back in the pre-Amelia days. I felt happy for the first time in a long time."

I closed my eyes and allowed myself to wallow in memories of Jonah. His smile, his hair, the weird way he brushed his teeth —each tooth individually and then the whole row from top to bottom and left to right. He was a meticulous tooth brusher and was rewarded for it every six months when he went to the dentist for a cleaning and the hygienist told him he had the least amount of plaque of any of her patients. Jonah proudly shared this information with me, and it became a standing joke between us. Whenever he forgot to put the toilet seat down or he placed dirty dishes in the dishwasher when the rest of them were clean I'd get annoyed and he'd reply that at least I'd married a man with plaque-free teeth and really, wasn't that more important? I smiled at the memory.

When I opened my eyes Dr. Rubenstein was staring at me. I expected her to ask me another question, but she didn't. She sat back in her chair and waited. Eventually, my thoughts shifted from memories of Jonah back to that night with Jake and my smile disappeared. "I can't even blame Jake since I was the one who initiated."

"Initiated how?"

"I kissed him right there at the dining room table."

"What was his reaction?"

"He kissed me back." What I didn't tell Dr. Rubenstein was that I'd never experienced so much longing before from just one kiss. Not even when Jonah was alive.

"I'm not sure which one of us suggested we go upstairs," I continued, "but it didn't matter because we both clearly wanted to."

"And you went to your bedroom?" Dr. Rubenstein asked. "The bedroom you used to share with Jonah?"

I nodded and the tears started flowing again. "You have to

understand. In that moment, in my head, he was Jonah. Going to our bedroom felt natural, not wrong."

"It wasn't wrong, Grace. Even if you were fully aware that you were with Jake and not Jonah, it still wouldn't be wrong."

I disagreed with her conclusion, but I continued. "It wasn't until we were almost naked that things started getting weird."

"Weird how?"

"You have to understand. Jonah and I had been together a long time. The sex between us was good but..."

"Predictable?" she offered.

I wasn't willing to concede that point. "Let's just say we weren't the most adventurous couple in the bedroom. But I was fine with that. We both knew what the other one liked and we stuck to the script. It worked for us."

"And Jake used a different script?"

"Very different," I said, thinking back to that night. "It's not that it was bad, it just wasn't Jonah. And that sort of brought me out of my stupor and I realized what I'd done. Or what I was about to do. And that's when I stopped."

"And how did Jake react when you stopped?"

I shrugged. "About how you'd expect. Not violent or anything, just confused. I mean, one minute I'm all over the guy and the next I'm pushing him away. Confusion was a reasonable response."

"And did you explain to him why you stopped?"

"God, no. I was mortified. And disgusted. Mostly with myself. I couldn't believe what I'd done, or what I'd almost done. When the reality of it hit me, I ran into the bathroom and puked up all the wine and pasta. I must've locked the door behind me because Jake kept banging on it asking me if I was okay. I kept telling him to leave, but I don't think he did."

"Why do you think that?"

"Because he's the one who found me. Although I suppose he could've left and come back, assuming he left the door unlocked. Honestly, I have no idea."

"You haven't spoken to him since that night?"

"No. He's called a couple of times, but I let it go to voicemail. I know my mom has spoken to him though, so he knows I'm okay."

I waited for Dr. Rubenstein to say something insightful, or empathetic, or just something that would relieve me of this horrible guilt. But when she finally spoke, all she said was, "I'm afraid our time is up."

I walked out into the sunshine feeling unmoored. Maybe slightly less guilty, but nowhere near absolved of my sins. And no way to avoid feeling these feelings I didn't want to feel.

I considered going back to my own house, but after last night's debacle with the bed I didn't want to. But I didn't want to sit in my aunt's house either. I glanced down at my sneakers. *I guess I could go for a walk.*

I DON'T KNOW how far I walked, but I ended up in a part of town I'd never been to before. Gone were the Starbucks and the Whole Foods and the overpriced boutiques that populated the downtown neighborhood where the Guest House was located. I was now in the un-gentrified section of Santa Veneta, where the houses had bars on the windows and the strip malls were filled with mini-markets and check cashing shops.

Out of habit I clutched my purse a little tighter, even though there was no one on the sidewalk but me. I was about to pass yet another no-name mini-market when I realized I was thirsty, so I stepped off the sidewalk and headed toward the entrance.

The wind picked up and I breathed in my favorite scent in

the world. I inhaled deeply and when I breathed out, I felt my shoulders drop several inches. It wasn't so much a decision as a compulsion. I had to discover the source of that intoxicating fragrance.

Chapter 11

"Can I help you?" the woman asked in heavily accented English. Her straight black hair was streaked with gray, but her olive skin was unlined. The petite Asian woman standing before me could've been forty-five or sixty-five, I had no idea.

"No, I'm good," I replied, then closed my eyes and inhaled deeply. I couldn't get enough of the fragrance. It smelled like childhood, it smelled like safety, it smelled like home.

"You need clothes cleaned?" she asked.

It was a reasonable question since I was standing in a coin-operated laundromat. Although according to the sign above the woman's head, they also offered fluff and fold service for $1.95 per pound.

"No." I inhaled again but less deeply this time lest the woman think I had some sort of breathing disorder.

"Then why you here?"

Again, another reasonable question. But one I had no answer to. "I stopped for a drink," I replied, realizing I never made it to the mini-market to purchase one. "Would you mind if I sat down for a minute? I'm a little tired." I motioned to the row of molded plastic chairs by the front windows. They were empty except for a large woman in bike shorts and a tank top (I assumed her more flattering outfits were in the washing machine), who was staring at her phone.

The Asian woman, who I guessed was the owner, or at least the manager, shrugged her shoulders and turned away.

It was a Tuesday afternoon, not prime laundry time, and the laundromat was mostly empty. Besides me, the proprietor, and the Lady in Lycra, there was only one other person in the shop —a girl wearing skintight jeans and a T-shirt. She looked like she should've been in high school but maybe classes had already ended for the day. She too was staring down at her phone. Only the proprietor glanced my way from time to time. It's possible she thought I was waiting for a score from my drug dealer. It was that kind of neighborhood.

I tried to look innocent as I sat on my plastic chair and inhaled. I'd forgotten how much I loved the scent of clean laundry, or more specifically, heavily scented laundry detergent. I didn't know the brand or the fragrance, but whatever it was, it smelled the same as the detergent my mom used when I was growing up. Or the same scent as the detergent my mom purchased. It was our housekeeper Anna who actually washed our dirty clothes and returned the clean ones to our closets and drawers.

When I was a little girl, Anna used to let me match the socks. When I was older, I helped fold. And before I left for college it was Anna who taught me how to wash my own clothes. She also taught me how to cook spaghetti and grilled cheese so I wouldn't starve when I lived on my own.

It was in college that I'd had to give up scented laundry detergent. I'd developed some sort of rash during my freshman year. It was probably stress related, or maybe just that coming from foggy San Francisco, I wasn't used to the drier climate in

Southern California. The doctor at the campus clinic suggested I eschew all fragrance and switch to unscented laundry detergent and skincare. I was never sure which product had been the culprit, or maybe none of them were and I just got used to college life, but the red, itchy bumps that had erupted all over my body disappeared and I've used only fragrance-free products since.

I was so used to unscented products that I now found most fragrances overpowering. But I still loved the smell of clean (scented) laundry. That has never left me.

I spotted a vending machine in the corner of the laundromat and purchased a Diet Coke. But when I returned to my molded plastic chair with the can of soda, the Asian woman came out from behind the counter and stood in front of me.

"You waiting for someone?"

"No."

"This not bus stop. Drop off laundry or leave."

"What if I wanted to do my laundry here? Not everyone drops off," I said, nodding to Skinny Jeans Girl who was transferring her wet clothes from the washer to the dryer. The Lady in Lycra was still scanning messages on her phone.

"You have clothes to wash?"

"Not on me. They're home."

"Then go home. This not place for you."

I couldn't deny that I looked out of place in this laundromat and not just because I was the only person not washing clothes. I considered arguing with her, but I figured if white people could call the cops on people of color for no reason at all, then people of color could call the cops on white people too. And while loitering in public was not a crime in California unless you also intended to commit a crime, which I didn't, I still slid my handbag onto my shoulder and walked outside.

That's when I noticed the empty storefront on the other

side of the laundromat—and the For Rent sign taped to the glass door.

Chapter 12

I PULLED my phone out of my purse and dialed the number on the sign.

"Yeah," a gruff voice answered on the fourth ring.

"Hi, I'm calling about the property for rent at—" I scanned the building for a street number but there wasn't one, and there was an empty pole on the corner where the street sign should've been. "It's on Rose in a strip mall next to a laundromat, not far from—"

"Yeah, what about it?"

"How much is it?"

"Why? You want to rent it?"

"Possibly."

"For what?"

I had no idea. All I knew was that I didn't want to leave this spot and the Asian lady was not going to let me loiter in her laundromat anymore. "A business."

"What kind of business?"

"Does it matter?"

"Yeah, it matters. Listen, lady, I don't know what you think you're doing, but let me set you straight. This ain't your kind of neighborhood."

Geez Louise. Is this what Black and brown people went through all the time? "You can tell that just by the sound of my voice? Don't you think that's a little racist?"

"Not your voice, sweetheart, I can tell by the look of you. And if that makes me a racist, so be it."

"You have no idea what I look like." This was an audio-only call.

"Turn around."

"Excuse me?"

"I said turn around."

I pivoted so instead of facing the empty storefront, I was looking at the auto mechanic shop across the street. Standing in the parking lot was an older white guy in greasy blue coveralls holding a cellphone to his ear. The man lifted his free hand and waved at me. "Mike Murphy."

"Grace. Grace Keegan-Hughes." I'd hyphenated when I'd married Jonah. Was I supposed to go back to just Keegan now that he was dead? And wasn't I supposed to be introducing myself as Charlie now too? Obviously, I wasn't very good at this.

"Nice to meet you, Grace Keegan-Hughes. Now tell me why a well-heeled lady such as yourself wants to set up shop in this neighborhood? You're not thinking of doing anything illegal, are you?"

"Of course not. I'm a lawyer."

"You want to hang out your shingle? In this part of town? What kind of lawyer are you?"

I really should've spent at least a few minutes thinking this through before I called. So I did what all my therapists thought I did best, I deflected. "Can you just tell me the price?"

He quoted me a monthly amount that seemed incredibly low. Although I'd worked in the litigation group of a huge national law firm when I'd lived in Los Angeles, when Jonah and I had moved to Santa Veneta, I'd had to take a job with a much smaller firm that did a little bit of everything, including commercial real estate. Therefore, I had some knowledge of local rents and that was by far the lowest amount I'd ever heard. Of course, I'd never worked on property leases in this neighborhood before.

"Will you do a six-month lease for that price?"

A six-month lease in commercial real estate was unheard of. The typical commercial property lease was three to five years, and some property owners only offered ten-year leases, at least when the market was booming and they could get away with it.

"Maybe," he said.

"Maybe?"

"Give me a few minutes to clean up. I'll come over and show you around."

It looked worse on the inside than it appeared from the outside. Someone had taped dark paper onto the front window so with the reflection from the sun it just looked like tinted glass. But under fluorescent lighting, there was no hiding the filth.

"I think the price you quoted me was too high," I said as our feet left dusty footprints in the threadbare carpet. I pointed to a red streak on the wall. "Is that blood?"

Mike shrugged. "Could be."

"It could be? Do you know that state law requires that you disclose to prospective tenants any deaths that occurred on the property in the last three years?"

"As far as I know the guy lived. Although he did end up in the hospital."

"As far as you know?"

"Hey, I don't keep track of my tenant's visitors. All I know is my former tenant's still alive because he's doing three to five in the state pen."

Lovely. "May I ask what your former tenant went to jail for?" I was hoping not manslaughter.

"Check kiting. And maybe a couple other things too. The S.O.B. still owes me five grand."

One corner of the black paper was already coming loose, so I pulled it the rest of the way down to let some sunlight in. It didn't make the office look any more attractive, but it did make the old stencil on the window visible. "Your former tenant was an accountant?"

Mike nodded. "Who better to kite checks?"

I could see his logic.

"I hope you're a criminal lawyer," Mike said. "'Cause that's what most folks around here need."

"Wow, that's ..." I was at a loss for words, something that rarely happened to me.

"What? You gonna accuse me of being a racist again?"

His comment felt racist, although I couldn't pinpoint why since he hadn't actually mentioned anyone's race. I realized it was because I was making the same assumptions about the people who lived in this neighborhood that he was. Did that make me a racist too? "Why are you assuming everyone who's poor is a criminal?"

"No, *you're* the one who's assuming. I've spent forty years in this neighborhood. I've seen it change from hard working people just trying to make a living to a bunch of drug dealers and prostitutes. And yes, they are mostly Black and Latino, although there's still a few lazy ass whites too. The Asians move in and out pretty quick. They got their own neighborhood a few miles east of here."

"What about the woman at the laundromat?"

"She's the exception. Hard worker, that one. She just got a

commercial contract for some of the restaurants downtown. Told me she's thinking of opening up a second location."

"I thought she was going to call the cops on me."

He let out a laugh. "She doesn't like loiterers."

"I was just resting."

"It's resting in your neighborhood. Around here it's loitering."

"You don't even know what neighborhood I live in."

He glanced down at my expensive sneakers and worked his way up my overpriced yoga pants, skimming my puffer vest, and landing at the designer sunglasses perched on top of my head. "I'm guessing The Hills."

I bristled. The Hills wasn't the official name of my neighborhood, but that's what everyone called the hillside area east of the freeway where Jonah and I and all our friends lived. "Usually, yes, but I happen to be living downtown at the moment."

Mike smiled wide. "Let me guess. One of those remodeled Craftsmans near the overpriced coffee shops. Or did you buy one of those fancy new condos across from the marina?"

I hated the look of those fancy new condos, but the Guest House was a remodeled Craftsman, and there was a Starbucks two blocks away. "What's your point, Mike?"

"My point is I know a lot more about this neighborhood and the people who live in it than you do."

"I'm sure you do. But crime can happen anywhere not just in the so-called 'bad neighborhoods,'" I said with the air quotes. That's when I realized this was the first time I'd thought about Jonah and Amelia since I'd left Dr. Rubenstein's office, probably a new record for me. While that realization gave me comfort, it depressed me too. I didn't want to forget about them.

"Yeah, porch pirates and people stealing the tires off your Tesla."

"We get violent crime in The Hills too."

He crossed his arms over his barrel chest. "Name one violent crime in your neighborhood in the past year."

Despite my well-documented aversion to sharing, with Mike I didn't hesitate. "Fourteen months ago, my husband and baby were shot on a busy street in broad daylight. No drug dealers, no prostitutes, just a crazy person with a gun."

Mike stopped smiling and his whole demeanor changed. "I remember that story. My wife, God rest her soul, talked about it for days. She couldn't stop thinking about that poor baby."

I could feel the tears welling up in my eyes. "Yeah, well..." I thought if I stopped talking maybe I could hold back the tears, but they spilled onto my cheeks anyway.

Mike had taken off the greasy coveralls before he'd crossed the street and now he reached into his jeans pocket and pulled out a crumpled tissue. He offered it to me, but I'd already fished one out of my purse. Even Before, I never left home without tissues. Allergies.

Mike stared up while I wiped my eyes and blew my nose. "I guess I could replace those missing tiles for you," he said, nodding at the open space in the corner of the ceiling. "And maybe paint the place."

"Oh, I don't know. The blood stain on the wall adds character, don't you think?"

We both laughed.

"This place needs more than paint, Mike. It needs to be fumigated. And the carpet is disgusting." I kicked at a threadbare patch, and it caught on my shoe.

"I'll replace the missing ceiling tiles and paint the place. The rest is on you."

"And the six-month lease?"

"You're not going to write me a bad check, are you?"

"I'm not going to write you a check at all. I assume you accept ACH transfers."

"Is that one of those money apps the bank's always pushing?"

"No, it's how you pay your bills online."

"I don't pay my bills online. I like paper, thank you very much."

I couldn't remember the last time I'd written out a paper check. But I was getting a great deal on this place, and I wasn't going to argue over the payment method. "If it's paper you want, it's paper you shall have." I held my hand out to Mike.

He stared at it a few seconds before he realized he was meant to shake it. His skin was rough, but his grip was looser than I'd thought it would be. Mike was the kind of man my father would've described as having a strong handshake. But he probably reserved that strong handshake for other men.

"I'll need a couple of days to fix up the place," he said. "You want to come by Friday morning and sign the lease?"

Was I actually going to rent this place? It was a crazy, impulsive decision and I didn't make crazy, impulsive decisions. Correction: Old Grace didn't make crazy, impulsive decisions. But after fourteen months of trying, I had to accept that there was no place for the Old Grace in After. If I was going to survive in After, I was going to have to embrace New Grace. Maybe New Grace made impulsive decisions all the time and it turned out great. There was only one way to find out.

Chapter 13

"ARE YOU CRAZY?" Aunt Maddy asked.

"Not crazy, just suicidally depressed." I smiled at Aunt Maddy, but she didn't smile back. "I honestly thought you'd be happy for me."

"If you told me you loved your new therapist and you were going to start seeing her three times a week, I'd be happy for you."

"Three times a week? Now that's crazy." I thought twice a week was a lot when Dr. Rubenstein had suggested it, but I'd agreed to try it for a month and then cut down to once a week, or maybe not at all if I didn't need her anymore.

"Or if you told me you were going back to your old job, I'd be happy for you."

"You know they replaced me ages ago." I didn't blame them. I'd already pushed the firm's limits with my six-month (unpaid) maternity leave. After Jonah's and Amelia's death, I had no idea when I'd be ready to go back to work.

"Did you even call them? Maybe they have another opening. Or maybe your boss knows of an opening somewhere else."

"I'm not calling my old firm."

"Why not?"

Because I had no desire to talk to anyone from Before. I'd run into one of my mommy-friends at the grocery store a few weeks after the funeral and it was incredibly awkward for both of us. Besides that she had no idea what to say to me, now that I was husbandless and childless, we had nothing in common anymore.

After the funeral, the only people I'd kept in touch with from Before were two former colleagues I used to socialize with outside the office. But even those relationships hadn't lasted. We met for drinks a couple of times, but I hated the pitying looks on their faces whenever Jonah's or Amelia's name came up. But it was even worse when they avoided mentioning Jonah and Amelia at all. It was as if they'd wanted to pretend they'd never existed. That's when I'd started turning down their invitations, and eventually they'd stopped inviting me. By that point I didn't care because I was busy with my advocacy work. I didn't have time for frivolous get-togethers. I had more important things to do. Until I didn't.

"I need a new project. Something I can sink my teeth into."

"You mean something to distract you from dealing with your loss."

I slammed my hands on the kitchen table and Aunt Maddy jumped. "Why is that so horrible? I'm doing what you and Mom want. I'm moving on with my life. You don't get to dictate how."

"Don't lump me in with your mother. She and I have very different opinions about this. She thinks being busy fixes everything. I don't."

"Well, you didn't like it when I was moping around the house all day. At least now I'll have somewhere to go."

Aunt Maddy shook her head and sighed. "Sweetie, don't be angry with me. You know I only want what's best for you. You just caught me off guard. Signing a lease on a whim because you liked the smell from the laundromat next door? You have to admit that's not like you."

I sighed too. "I know, but I don't know what to do anymore. My whole life I've planned and analyzed and looked before I leaped and it all ended in disaster."

"It was random bad luck, Grace. No amount of planning can prevent that."

"I know. That's why I need to try something new. You know, when I was at the Wellstone Center I actually thought about changing my name."

"To what?" she asked.

"Charlie, short for Charlotte."

"I'm not calling you Charlie."

I laughed. "I know. It sounds weird to me too. I was just desperate to start over. To live a different life. To be someone else."

"You don't need to *be* someone else," Aunt Maddy said, "you need to *do* something else."

"Exactly! I need to do things differently."

"Different? Yes. Crazy? No."

"Why is renting an office and starting my own firm crazy?"

"Well, for one thing, you don't have any clients."

"You had no guests when you bought this place and that didn't stop you."

"As I recall, you and your mother both thought the idea of me buying this house and turning it into a B&B was crazy."

"And we were both wrong. You did what you thought was right and it worked out for you. Why can't I do the same?"

Aunt Maddy sighed again and I could tell she was softening.

"Just tell me this, Grace. Will starting your own firm give you peace?"

I shrugged. "It's only a six-month lease."

Chapter 14

I GLANCED over at Aunt Maddy, who'd insisted on driving us to my new office. "We don't need to do this. I'm not signing the lease until tomorrow."

"I know," she said. "I just want to see the place before you decide."

"I've already decided. It's a done deal."

"You're the lawyer. You know it's not a done deal until the lease is signed."

I sighed. My mom called last night to see how I was doing aka check up on me. Unlike Aunt Maddy, my mother was thrilled when I told her I was opening my own law firm. She was less thrilled when Aunt Maddy told her where that law firm would be located. I think she enlisted Aunt Maddy's help to get me to change my mind. Hence, the trip to the new office today.

I directed Aunt Maddy to the strip mall and she pulled into a parking spot in front of the laundromat. As soon as I opened my car door I inhaled. "Don't you just love that smell?"

She shrugged. "If I knew you liked it so much, I would've

bought you a scented candle. It would've saved us all a lot of aggravation."

I laughed. "You think Jonah and Amelia would be alive today if only you'd bought me a scented candle?"

Aunt Maddy nodded to the empty storefront that was soon to be mine. "This isn't going to bring them back, Grace."

"I know that. But I need to do something with my days. Please support me on this."

Aunt Maddy shook her head and pulled open the glass door.

I was surprised by all the activity. Mike was up on a ladder installing new ceiling tiles, two men in paint-spattered clothes were rolling off-white paint onto the walls and there was a third man pulling up the carpet.

"I thought the carpet was on me," I said to Mike.

He turned his head in my direction but didn't climb down. "I'm just pulling it up for you. You can do what you want."

I turned to Aunt Maddy. "See how accommodating he is. I'd never find a landlord that accommodating in a nice part of town."

Aunt Maddy snorted.

"Who's your friend?" Mike asked.

"This is my Aunt Madeline. Aunt Maddy, Mike Murphy."

Mike half turned on the ladder. "Nice to meet you."

"One question for you, Mr. Murphy. Why are you taking advantage of a grieving widow?"

Mike's eyebrows shot up. "I, um—"

"What the hell, Aunt Maddy?"

"C'mon, Grace. How far are you going to take this?"

"Excuse us a minute," I said to Mike, then pulled Aunt Maddy outside.

It was one of the worst fights we'd ever had, and it didn't end even when one of the workmen opened the front door and strolled past us with the rolled-up carpet on his shoulder. His arrival just caused us to lower our voices.

"I know you don't approve of what I'm doing and I don't care. I'm a grown woman. I don't need your permission."

"A grown woman who tried to kill herself last week," Aunt Maddy hissed. "Maybe you're not in the best mental space right now to be making long-term decisions."

"It's a six-month lease!"

The front door opened again; Mike this time. "Sorry to interrupt, but are you going to want to divide up this room? Because if you are, I should tell the painters. Unless you're going to paint the new wall yourself."

"Um." I hadn't thought that far ahead, but it was actually a good idea. I'd want an office in the back of the space with a door that I could close so I could talk to clients in private and a reception area in the front. Not that I had a receptionist yet, or clients. But I did have money, thanks to Jonah's life insurance policies.

"Yes, I'll need an office in the back. Do you happen to know anyone who can build me a wall?"

"I'm sure I can find someone," Mike said.

"That won't be necessary," Aunt Maddy replied. And before I could object, she added, "I know a guy. But she'll need security cameras too and lights with motion detectors. I assume there's a parking space for her in the back."

"Two spaces," Mike replied. "Four if the cars are small and you're okay with tandem parking."

"Good." Aunt Maddy pulled her keys out of her purse. "We'll be back later with the equipment, if you would be so kind as to install it for us."

"I suppose I could do that," Mike replied.

Aunt Maddy nodded and turned back to me. "C'mon. We have some shopping to do."

"I don't understand," I said, after we'd both shut our car doors. "You just spent the last twenty minutes trying to talk me out of this and now you're helping me?"

"Remember when you were ten and you led that sit-in at school because they took Tater Tots off the hot lunch menu?"

I laughed. "Oh my god, I totally forgot about that. Mom was really pissed at me. I only got suspended from school for a day, but she grounded me for a month!"

"Well, I saw that same determination on your face just now that I saw back then, and I knew no matter what I said you were going through with this. So if I can't stop you, the least I can do is make sure you're safe. Nothing's foolproof, but outdoor lights and security cameras will put my mind at ease, and your mother's too."

"Thank you, Aunt Maddy. I knew there was a reason you were my favorite aunt."

"I'm your *only* aunt."

"That too."

AUNT MADDY'S guy couldn't build the new wall until the middle of next week, but that gave us time to sand down and paint the concrete floor and buy some furniture. A week after the lease was signed, I had a functional office space but still no clients.

Malcolm Juan Wilson's timing couldn't have been better.

Chapter 15

I was sitting on my new mint green sofa in my week-old reception area, reading the news on my phone and enjoying the clean laundry scent that wafted in from the laundromat next door when the front door banged open.

"You fixed this place up real nice," the boy said as he ambled in.

"Uh, thanks." He couldn't have been more than fifteen years old, probably younger, and he had that swagger that only teenage boys (and presumably their female counterparts) think makes them look cool, but is laughable to everyone else. "Can I help you?"

He reached for one of the two armless chairs leaning against the opposite wall, set it down in front of me, spun it around, and sat with his legs straddling the seat. "It's not about what you can do for me, but what I can do for you."

I couldn't help myself. I laughed out loud. "Is this a joke?"

He seemed genuinely offended. "This ain't no joke."

"Okay, calm down. No offense intended." He was a kid, but a tall kid who despite being skinny could easily take me in a fight. It was just the two of us in my office.

"I ain't offended. Mike told me to come over here and talk to you."

"Mike? Mike Murphy?" I glanced out the front window at the A-1 Auto Repair shop across the street. I saw several cars parked in the lot, but no Mike.

"Yeah. I work for him sometimes. I'm the one who scraped the last guy's sign off your window."

"You did a good job." There was no trace of the lettering and the glass was streak free.

"I'm good at lots of things. Mike thought you might want to hire me."

This time I clamped down on my laughter. "Hire you? To do what, exactly?"

"Whatever you want. I can answer your phone, run errands, type shit up. I'm real good on the computer. I used to work for a guy who fixed them so I know how to do that too. I can do whatever you need."

"How old are you?" I asked.

He lifted his chin. "Sixteen."

"You are not sixteen. I doubt you're even fifteen." And then it occurred to me that it was still morning. "Why aren't you in school?"

"Damn school's closed for teacher training or some shit like that. Ain't they supposed to be trained already? I thought you had to go to college to be a teacher."

"Wow, it sounds like you actually like school."

He shrugged. "'S okay."

A teenage boy who thinks he's a player but is willing to do any kind of work and he actually likes going to school? Something about this kid didn't add up. "What's your name?"

"Malcolm. But everyone calls me MJ."

"Nice to meet you, MJ. I'm Grace."

He nodded. "So you gonna hire me or what?"

The kid was direct, I'd give him that. "What did Mike tell you about me? Did he tell you that I was a lawyer?"

"No shit," he said. "For real?"

"For real. You want to see my Bar card?"

"No man, it's cool. I was thinking I might want to be a lawyer someday."

"Oh yeah, what kind of lawyer?" I had a suspicion I was being played.

"The kind you see on TV, except I'll be getting people out of jail. 'Cause guys who look like me get a raw deal and that shit ain't right."

He was correct that in our criminal justice system Black and brown boys were convicted at higher rates and received longer sentences than white boys accused of the same crimes. But I doubted MJ had read the statistics. He didn't have to. He lived them. "So you want to be a public defender?"

"Is that the crappy lawyer they give you when you got no money?"

Not how I would've described it, but, "Yes."

"No, I'm gonna wear a dope suit and drive around town in my Mercedes," he said, pretending he had his hands on a steering wheel. "Those free lawyers don't make shit."

I laughed. "Well, you're right about that. But most of those high-priced defense lawyers you see on TV actually started out in the DA's office—those are the lawyers who put people in jail. After a while, unless they plan on going into politics, they switch sides and start defending white collar criminals who can afford to pay for their nice Mercedes and their dope suits."

"So you're saying if I want to make lots of money, I gotta put people in jail first?"

"I'm afraid so. Or, at least, that's how it's usually done. Maybe you can find a different path."

He seemed to give this serious consideration. "I guess I

could just put the really bad ones in jail. Like the guys who hurt kids."

Interesting that was the example he chose. I couldn't help but wonder why. "Yes, there are attorneys who specialize in that kind of thing."

"That'd be okay then."

"Good. But since I'm already a lawyer and you're going to be one someday, I think we both need to follow the law. Which means I can't even think about hiring you unless I know how old you are. So be honest with me, MJ, are you really sixteen?"

He stared down at the floor and said, "Fifteen last week." He looked up. "But I've been mowing lawns since I was ten."

"Yes, but I'm pretty sure those people whose lawns you mowed weren't paying taxes on your wages and neither were you. When you work for Mike, does he pay you in cash or by check?"

"Cash."

I figured. He probably just hired the kid to help him out. I was sure Mike was capable of scraping the stenciled letters off my front window himself.

"I can't do that, MJ. If I hired you, I'd have to do it legally. There are labor laws that restrict what jobs you can do and what hours you can work if you're under sixteen."

"Okay, I'll work whenever you want. I'll even pay taxes and shit."

I laughed again. "I'm sure that will make the IRS happy."

"So I'm hired?"

"Um." I really had no need for an employee since at the moment I had no clients and no work to do. But I liked MJ. He made me laugh. And it might be nice having company in the office. I was getting bored just reading the news and social media all day. "Let me think about it. Come back Monday after school and we'll talk."

His face broke into a huge grin. "Sure thing, Grace." He put the chair back against the wall without me having to ask and swaggered out of my office.

I waited until MJ was out of sight before I locked my front door and walked across the street. I found Mike standing underneath a car raised high on a lift. Both his coveralls and his hands were covered in black streaks.

"Got a minute?" I shouted over the sounds coming from the next bay where a man I'd never seen before was pulling tires off an old Honda.

"Do I look like I got a minute?" he said, still staring up at the dark underbelly of the car above our heads.

"I wanted to talk to you about MJ."

"He's a good kid," he said, reaching into the engine. Or maybe it was the transmission. I had no idea. "You should hire him."

"Hire him as what?"

Mike finally pulled his attention away from the car's insides and looked at me. "How should I know? I have no idea what you do all day. Not much from what I've seen."

I knew I shouldn't be offended, but I was. "What is that supposed to mean?"

"Nothing. It's just that I haven't seen a lot of visitors to your *office*."

It was the emphasis on the word office that really set me off. "Who the hell are you to judge? You have no idea what I do in my *office* all day."

"Exactly. That's what I just said."

And somehow that statement defused the budding argument. "Okay. About MJ, why did you send him to me?"

"Because he's a good kid who needs a job."

"And you thought I needed an employee?"

"MJ's lived here his whole life; knows everyone in the neighborhood. And his uncle's a bigtime drug dealer in LA. I bet *he* could use a good lawyer."

"I'm not a criminal defense lawyer, Mike. I was a civil litigator in LA, and when I moved up to Santa Veneta, I started doing corporate work and real estate."

"Not much call for corporate lawyers around here. Maybe you should go back to The Hills."

Not that BS again. I folded my arms across my chest and stared at him.

"Hey, I'm just your landlord. You owe me six months' rent whether you got any clients or not. I just thought maybe you and MJ could help each other out. Isn't that why you set up shop here? You're one of those do-gooders who wants to help people?"

Chapter 16

"It's a good question, Grace," Dr. Rubenstein said at our appointment that afternoon. "Because it's not clear to me what you're trying to achieve with this endeavor."

"I told you. I liked the laundry smell."

Dr. Rubenstein actually snorted—and I didn't think therapists were allowed to do that. "Don't bullshit a bullshitter, Grace. If it was just about the scent, you could've bought some detergent and gone home and done your own laundry."

"I'm allergic to the fragrance."

"Then you could've gotten a job at a laundromat and washed other people's clothes for a living."

"I just said I liked the scent not the endless sorting and folding." That was one aspect of parenting I definitely disliked. I'd never washed so many clothes before as I had after Amelia was born. She was constantly spitting up on herself and me too.

Dr. Rubenstein leaned back in her Eames chair and sighed.

"I just needed a place to go during the day. I'm not allowed to move back to my own house, and if I had to hang around my aunt's place all day trying to look happy and not at all suicidal, I really would lose my mind."

71

"Why didn't you just get a job? Wouldn't that be easier than starting your own business?"

"I don't want to work for anyone else anymore. I want to have some control over my life."

Dr. Rubenstein nodded. "Now I understand."

I was glad she did, because I was having doubts. It had been fun buying furniture and decorating the place with Aunt Maddy. And I agreed with my mom and my aunt that it was good for me to leave the house every day. It meant I had to shower and get dressed every morning, which was more than I'd been doing for the past fourteen months. I'd even gotten into the habit of walking up to Starbucks for a coffee even though I could've easily made my own at home.

But once I arrived at my office each day, I had no idea what to do with myself. I didn't have a clue how to find clients. Hell, I wasn't even sure what type of law I was practicing anymore.

"I understand your desire for control, Grace. And I commend you for taking action. That's a huge step. But the process normally works better if you have some idea of what you want to accomplish. I know you don't believe in making plans anymore, but you need a goal, at least in the short-term."

"Well, I'd like to have a client."

"Great. What do you intend to do for this client?"

And that's where the goal-making hit a wall. "Whatever they need?"

"Okay, but can you narrow it down a bit? For example, I assume you'll be offering this client legal services of some type?"

"Sure."

"What type of legal services? Do you prepare wills? Or write contracts? Or go to court?"

"All the above. Except the wills. Estate planning is a very specialized area of the law and not something I know much about, although I suppose I could learn."

"Is that what you want to do? Learn how to prepare wills?"

"No, drafting wills all day sounds really boring. Plus, I'm guessing most poor people don't really need wills since you only need a will if you have something of value to leave behind."

"So you're working exclusively for poor people now? Because that's not what you did before, right?"

"Right. But that's the point. I'm not the same person I was before...the accident." It was easier to refer to it as an accident instead of a murder. Accidents happen. Murders aren't supposed to. "I'm New Grace."

"And what does New Grace do? Or what does she want to do?"

That was the million dollar question.

WHAT DOES NEW GRACE DO? That was the thought running through my head as I drove back to my office. I knew that New Grace was a lawyer. But beyond that I had no idea. My mission was to find out.

Chapter 17

I WASN'T sure what time school let out or even which school MJ attended, but I figured he'd swagger into my office sometime after two on Monday afternoon, so I made sure I was there waiting for him. When he hadn't arrived by four o'clock I locked the front door and stomped across the street. I found Mike bent over the open hood of a silver sedan.

"MJ never showed."

Mike glanced up at me then quickly returned his attention back to the car's engine.

"Well? Aren't you going to say something?"

"What do you want me to say? He's not here either."

"Do you know where he is?"

"Why would I know where he is? I'm not his keeper."

"You're the one who recommended him to me. I think you have some responsibility here."

Mike wiped his hands on a rag and stood up. "You're nuts, you know that?"

No, just suicidally depressed, I thought but didn't say. "I told him to come back after school today and he never showed."

"Maybe something came up."

"Like what?"

"How would I know," he said, clearly exasperated. "If you're so interested, go ask him."

"I think I will," I replied and whipped my phone out of my purse. "What's his number?"

"Last time I saw him he didn't have a cell. And I wouldn't count on the home phone working either."

"Why not?"

"Because the phone company turns it off when you don't pay the bill. They're picky that way."

"Can you at least give me his address?"

"Yeah, but I don't think you want to go there by yourself and I haven't got time to escort you."

"I don't need an escort, Mike, I just need an address."

I SHOULDN'T HAVE BEEN SO CAVALIER about the escort. I wasn't scared when I passed a group of guys standing on the corner passing money and baggies between them, but the homeless guy ranting at his invisible enemy did make me wish I'd driven the four blocks to MJ's apartment instead of walking. And when a group of teenage boys called out to me in Spanish and then laughed amongst themselves as I walked past, I picked up my pace.

I stopped when I reached the beige two-story apartment building surrounded by a black iron fence, which was virtually indistinguishable from the other two story apartment buildings that filled this neighborhood. There was a lock on the front gate, but someone had left the door propped open with a rock, so I walked into the yard and up the steps to unit number eight.

MJ answered the door in the same jeans and T-shirt he'd been wearing the day I met him. I'd been expecting a friendly greeting, maybe even an apology for blowing me off. Instead I got an angry, "What are you doing here?"

So I replied with an equally angry, "Looking for you. Can I come in?"

MJ didn't invite me in, but he didn't try to block me either. I hadn't seen an apartment this filthy since college. There was a huge water stain on the popcorn ceiling, the carpet looked like it hadn't been vacuumed in months, and the faux wood grain coffee table was barely visible under the pile of used paper plates and grease-stained take-out bags. All that was missing from the dorm room chic was the empty pizza box.

"You live here?" I asked, even though I knew the answer.

MJ nodded.

"Why didn't you come back today? I thought you wanted a job."

"I do want a job."

"Well, no one's going to hire you if you don't show up for work on your first day!"

I was expecting an excuse, but MJ just stared down at the dirty carpet. I didn't know what to do. I wanted to help him, but I couldn't if he wouldn't tell me what was going on.

"Okay, MJ. I don't think this is going to work out." I turned to leave but stopped when I heard a girl's voice call his name. "Who's that?" I asked.

"Nobody," MJ said to the floor, refusing to look at me.

I was about to investigate when a little girl appeared in the doorway to what I presumed was the bedroom. Her skin was a few shades lighter than MJ's, and she was wearing a pink nightgown that barely covered her knees and one dingy white sock. Her long dark hair was in disarray and her legs were covered in red bumps, some of which were scabbed over as if she'd scratched them and made them bleed.

"Who is that?" I asked again.

"My sister. Sofia."

I trooped to the back of the apartment and kneeled down on the stained carpet so I was eye-level with the little girl. "Hi, Sofia. I'm Grace. I'm a friend of your brother's. Are you okay?"

She looked past me to MJ as if asking permission to speak. I grabbed her hand to get her attention. It was so hot and clammy that I immediately placed my other hand on her forehead. She was burning up. I let go of Sofia and spun around. "Did you know she has a fever?"

MJ nodded. "The babysitter left me a note."

"Left you a note? You mean she just left Sofia here alone?"

"Yeah, she didn't want her getting the other kids sick."

"Who the hell is this woman?" Whoever she was, she shouldn't be responsible for watching anyone's children. I considered calling the police. I didn't know what was going on here, but whatever it was, I knew it wasn't good. "Where's your mother?"

"Can you just leave?" MJ said.

"Not until you tell me where your mother is."

"Work. Then Sofia got sick and—"

That's all he'd managed to say before Sofia puked all over the floor. The vomit missed my pants but splashed onto my shoes.

"Sorry," she said before the tears started streaming down her face.

"It's okay, Sofia, don't cry," I replied as MJ ran over with a handful of used paper napkins.

"What am I supposed to do with these? Get me the paper towels."

"We don't got any paper towels."

"Then go get me a regular towel."

I carefully lifted the soiled nightgown over Sofia's head and handed it to MJ. He ran into what I presumed was the bathroom and returned with a thin blue towel that was hard to the touch and smelled like it hadn't been washed in weeks. But it was large enough for me to wipe up the vomit.

"Go get her some clean clothes," I said as I took the towel into the bathroom and rinsed it in the sink, which was as dirty as the rest of the house. I peeked in the medicine cabinet while I was there, which was empty but for a bottle of aspirin and a box of no-name bandages.

"Where's your thermometer?" I called out to MJ.

"I don't know," he called back from the next room.

I didn't need a thermometer. I knew Sofia had a fever just by touching her. I hung the towel over the shower rod, rinsed out the soiled nightgown and hung that too, then joined MJ and Sofia in the bedroom. There were piles of clothes everywhere, plus a backpack and a few school books, which I assumed were MJ's. Sofia laid on a mattress on the floor and MJ sat next to her holding her hand.

"Do you have any medicine? Children's Tylenol or Motrin?"

"There's aspirin in the bathroom, but I know you're not supposed to give that to little kids."

I was glad he knew that much. "Okay, get her some pants and shoes." MJ had changed her into a T-shirt that hung down to her knees, I guessed one of his. "I'll be back soon."

"Where you going?" he asked.

"To get my car."

"Why?"

"Well, you don't think we're staying here, do you?"

Chapter 18

I CALLED Amelia's pediatrician's office on the drive over. I still had the number programmed into my phone. The nurse who answered remembered me.

"You had another child, Mrs. Hughes? That's wonderful."

"She's not mine. I'm just taking care of her. I know you close soon, but she has a fever and she's vomiting. Is there any way you could possibly squeeze her in this afternoon?"

"If you can get here before five. And please use the back entrance so she doesn't get the rest of the children sick."

"Will do," I said and hung up.

"You can get an appointment just like that?" MJ asked.

He was sitting in the back seat next to Sofia. Technically, we were breaking the law since Sofia should've been strapped into a booster seat. But I knew if I'd stopped at the store first to buy one, we'd never make it to the pediatrician's office before they closed.

"Not a check-up appointment," I said, "but if your child's sick, then yes, they'll usually squeeze you in."

"The last time I went to the doctor we had to wait in the ER all night."

"You should never go to the ER unless it's an actual emergency, MJ. You're wasting limited resources."

"But Mama says they have to take you at the ER, even if you can't pay."

I wanted to crawl under the seat. Of course that's why his mother took him to the ER. For people without health insurance, it was the only option. My privilege was showing again. If I was going to start representing poor people instead of giant corporations, I'd have to work on that.

After a long pause MJ said, "I don't got no money. I can't pay the doctor."

"I know, MJ. This one's on me."

Doctor Ensley didn't ask a lot of questions about how Sofia ended up in my care. I signed the consent form and the office staff accepted it. Dr. Ensley was more concerned with Sofia's physical condition and the fact that neither MJ nor I could answer even the most basic questions about Sofia's medical history.

"It's probably just a virus," Doctor Ensley said when she'd completed her exam. "There's a nasty bug going around. Alternate acetaminophen and ibuprofen to get the fever down and make sure she's getting plenty of fluids. You don't want her to get dehydrated. And if her temperature goes higher call me and we'll figure out next steps. In the meantime, you need to talk to whoever she's been taking care of her and get her medical history. And tell them they need to call an exterminator. The poor kid's covered in flea bites."

Target was only half a mile away so we drove there next. I didn't really want to take Sofia into the store in case she got sick again, so MJ waited with her in the car with all the windows rolled down. (I'd insisted he open the windows even though the sun was setting and there was no danger of them suffocating in the heat). I hurried through the aisles, grabbing Sofia's medicine and a booster seat and, on impulse, a stuffed bear too. By the time I completed my purchase and returned to the car, both kids were asleep. I considered taking them to my house since it was closer, but I didn't want Aunt Maddy to worry about me and this situation was too complicated to easily explain over the phone.

I wasn't sure how Aunt Maddy would react to two kids spending the night at her place, especially since one of them was sick, and I was definitely not looking forward to explaining how they ended up in my care. But as soon as I spotted the black Audi parked out front, I was glad I had MJ and Sofia with me. They would save me from having to talk to the person I'd been avoiding for weeks.

Chapter 19

"You brought friends," Aunt Maddy said when the three of us walked into the living room. I'd woken both kids when we'd arrived, but poor Sofia could barely stand. I would've carried her, but she was too heavy for me to hold for more than a minute or two, so I held on tightly to her clammy hand and tried to keep her upright.

"This is MJ," I said, nodding in his direction, "and this is Sofia," I added, lifting our conjoined hands. "This is my Aunt Maddy—and Jake."

Aunt Maddy fed MJ dinner while I gave Sofia a bath. I asked Sofia questions about her mother, the babysitter, where she went to school, but she was so sleepy she could barely keep her eyes open. Coherent answers was too much to expect, so after she finished bathing I helped her back into her clothes and tucked her into bed in the Starfish Room. I'd sleep in a different room tonight.

"How do you all know each other?" Jake asked when I joined the three of them at the dining room table. MJ was on either his second or third helping of Aunt Maddy's lasagna, but Jake and Aunt Maddy had waited for me to join them before they started to eat.

MJ stopped inhaling his cheesy pasta and turned to me.

I would've preferred to explain the situation to Aunt Maddy privately, but Jake didn't appear to be leaving anytime soon. "I opened my own law firm and MJ works for me. Sofia's his sister."

"Whoa," Jake said, "When did all this happen?"

"Recently," I replied.

"Don't you think it's a little soon?" Jake asked.

"Soon?" MJ said.

MJ wasn't talking, but he was clearly listening to every word.

I took a deep breath and turned to MJ. "I don't know if Mike told you, but my husband and daughter were killed last year." I knew Jake was referring to my suicide attempt, not their deaths, but that was not a topic I was prepared to discuss with MJ.

"Oh," MJ said. "Sorry."

"Thanks." I smiled, then Aunt Maddy redirected the conversation to MJ and that's how we found out that he was a freshman at Santa Veneta High School and that Sofia was five years old but hadn't started kindergarten yet.

"When did she turn five?" I asked.

"Last summer," MJ said. "Her birthday's in July."

"Why isn't she in school yet?" Obviously, their home life wasn't ideal, but I would've thought their mother would've wanted to enroll Sofia in school, for the free childcare if for no other reason.

MJ shrugged.

"Did your mom think she wasn't ready yet?" Aunt Maddy asked.

"I guess so," MJ said, directing his words at his now-empty plate.

My aunt and I exchanged a glance.

"MJ," I said, "where is your mom?" I knew I should've pushed him for an answer sooner, but it had been so crazy rushing to the pediatrician's office before they closed, and to the store for medicine, and then my aunt's house that I felt like I was just now catching my breath.

"Work," he said, still looking down.

"Where does she work?" Aunt Maddy asked. When MJ didn't answer, she said, "You should really call her. She's probably worried sick about you."

I pulled my cell out of my purse and held it out to him. "Here, you can use my phone."

He shook his head. "No, she works late. She doesn't even know we're gone."

I set my phone on the table next to his plate. "MJ, we need to talk to your mother. Please call her."

"She's not allowed to get calls at work," he said and finally looked up. "I'm done. Can I leave now?"

Aunt Maddy and I exchanged another glance before I said, "If by leave you mean be excused from the table, then yes. Why don't you go upstairs and check on Sofia. Her room's at the end of the hall to the left. I'll be up in a minute and we can figure out which you'll sleep in."

"I'll just sleep with Sofia," he said.

"You can't," Aunt Maddy replied. "Her room only has one bed."

"That's okay. We sleep together all the time."

Aunt Maddy shot me another look. I knew she thought it was inappropriate for a teenage boy to be sharing a bed with a young girl, but she hadn't seen their apartment.

"I know, MJ, but Sofia's sick and I don't want you to get sick too."

"Then I'll sleep on the floor."

"No one's sleeping on the floor," Aunt Maddy replied. "We have plenty of beds in this house. If you want to be near your sister, I'll get you a rollaway."

"What's a rollaway?" MJ asked.

"C'mon, I'll show you," Jake said. It was the first time he'd spoken directly to MJ. He'd spent most of the meal silently eating his lasagna and sipping his wine.

When Jake and MJ headed out to the garage to find the rollaway bed, I stood up and started clearing dishes. I didn't wait for Aunt Maddy to ask. "I know you have questions."

"There's an understatement."

"But I have questions too. Why is Jake here?"

"He came to see you," she said, following me into the kitchen with a stack of dirty salad bowls. "He said you won't return his calls. Your mother told him you were staying with me. Want to answer my questions now?"

"Let me get MJ settled first," I said. "Then I'll explain everything. I promise."

When I walked into the Starfish Room, MJ and Jake had already set up the rollaway bed and were tucking the sheet around the mattress. With two beds in the small room, there was barely enough space for all three of us to stand.

"You can shower before bed if you want," I said quietly, not wanting to wake Sofia. Although she hadn't woken when they'd carried in the rollaway or turned on the overhead light, so I was probably worrying for nothing. "There are clean towels under the sink and I'll find you a toothbrush." I was sure Aunt Maddy had extras somewhere.

MJ sat down on the rollaway and kicked off his sneakers without untying the laces. "Nah, I'm good."

This time I exchanged a glance with Jake, who placed his hand on MJ's shoulder. "Grace is too nice to tell you, but I'm not. You stink, bro. Now get your ass in the shower so the rest of us can breathe."

I didn't disagree with the sentiment, only the delivery. "Cut him some slack, Jake. It's been a tough day."

Jake spun around and wagged his finger at me. "And you've got some explaining to do."

MJ leapt up from the bed with his fists clenched and positioned himself between me and Jake. "Grace don't have to tell you nothing, if she don't want to."

I was touched by MJ's response. And it made me wonder if he'd had to defend other women in his life too.

"It's *doesn't*, not don't," Jake replied with his jaw clenched. Jonah used to clench his jaw when he was angry too.

"Whatever," MJ replied.

Before Jake could respond I reached for MJ's shoulder and turned him so he was facing me instead of Jake. "What size do you wear?"

"Why?" he asked.

"You've been wearing that same shirt for three days." And possibly longer considering how pungent he was. "I want to buy you some clean clothes."

"Nah, I'm good. I have more clothes at home."

Unwashed, I assumed, from the unkempt piles on the floor of his apartment. "I know, but I don't feel like driving all the way back to your place tonight. I'll just go to Target. Nothing fancy, I promise." I knew he was worried about the money. He'd already insisted he was going to pay me back for the doctor visit, even though I told him it wasn't necessary.

He said no twice more before he relented. He headed into

the bathroom to shower and I headed downstairs with Jake following. I stuck my head in the living room where Aunt Maddy was watching TV. "Dessert?" she asked. "I picked up cupcakes at Daisy's."

She was doing her best to fatten me up. She knew I loved Daisy's cupcakes and her lasagna too.

"When I get back. I'm just running out to Target to pick up a few things for MJ and Sofia."

"Oh? Will they be staying with us long?"

"Not long," I said, even though I really had no idea. "But they need clean clothes for the morning. Don't worry, I'll be back soon." I sprinted out the front door before she could ask any more questions.

I wasn't surprised when Jake followed me outside. I knew he wanted answers, and not just about MJ and Sofia. "You don't need to come. I know you hate shopping." Jonah was the same.

"I have to come," he said. "You need me."

"I do?"

"Yes. You have no idea what teenage boys wear."

He was right about that. Although I figured I couldn't go wrong with a pair of jeans and a T-shirt. I was uncertain about the pajamas. Jonah always slept in his boxers, but he was a grown man. Did teenage boys sleep in their underwear too? And if so, did they wear boxers or briefs?

Jake insisted on driving. It was both an odd and a familiar sensation for me to sit in the passenger seat of the Audi. The last time I'd sat in this seat was when Jonah was alive. The Audi had been his car then. I'd given it to Jake after Jonah died.

As soon as Jake screeched away from the curb, the interrogation began.

Chapter 20

"Why won't you return my calls?" Jake demanded.

It could have been worse. He could've started with why I kissed him, then kicked him out of my bed, then tried to kill myself, all in the same night. But since he started small, I did too. "You know why."

"No, Grace, I really don't. I have no idea why you won't talk to me. What did I do wrong? I mean, the last time I saw you, you tried to kill yourself. What the hell?"

And there it was. "I'm sorry. Sorry that I put you through that and sorry I haven't returned your calls. I just didn't know what to say."

"An explanation would be nice."

I didn't want to hurt his feelings, but I didn't see any way out of this. "I never meant to lead you on. Please know that. I was just so out of my mind that night. I didn't even realize it was you I was with."

"Bullshit. You knew it was me."

"Later I did. That's why I stopped. But not at first."

"You did too. You called me by my name."

I didn't remember doing that, but even if I had, "Jake, you're Jonah's brother. It never should've happened."

"Why not? Jonah's gone. You need to accept that."

"I have accepted it. But that doesn't make what we did right."

"What's wrong with what we did? You wanted me, and I wanted you too. It's perfectly natural."

"I wanted Jonah, not you."

"No, Grace, you wanted *me*."

I rolled my eyes. The giant Jake Hughes ego. He couldn't imagine a woman *not* wanting him, even his own sister-in-law. Thankfully, this was a trait he and Jonah didn't share. "Okay, Jake. Believe what you want to believe."

That's when he slammed on the brakes. Luckily, the traffic was light and the shoulder of the highway was empty. Otherwise, we surely would've gotten into an accident. "What the fuck?"

"We need to talk about this."

"No, we need to get to Target before it closes and that's all we need to do."

"Not until you admit the truth."

"What truth?"

"You knew it was me in your bed that night and you panicked. You felt guilty. I understand. But, Grace, you have nothing to feel guilty about. Jonah would want you to move on."

"Not with you!"

"I disagree. Jonah would want me to be there for you, to take care of you. And it's not as if that was our first kiss."

I couldn't believe he was bringing that up. It was true that I'd kissed Jake prior to that night, but it was before I'd ever met Jonah! A friend of mine had dragged me out to a bar near campus, which is where I'd met Jake. When I decided to leave, he offered

89

to walk me to my car, which was parked down the block, and we kissed. But's that all we did. When he invited me to a party at his house the following weekend, I accepted. Jake was attractive (and a good kisser) so I figured why not. And that's where I met Jonah.

Jonah shared Jake's good looks, but that's where the similarities ended. I spent hours talking to Jonah and when he asked me for my phone number, I gave it to him. Our first date was dinner and a movie the following weekend. After that we were together until the day he died.

"I don't know how else to say this, Jake, so I'm just going to say it. I am not interested in dating you. Not now, not ever."

After a few seconds of silence, he asked, "Who said anything about dating? I thought you just wanted sex."

And before I could lay into him he shot me the Hughes smile, the one that always got Jonah out of trouble too. "You're an arrogant jerk, you know that?"

Jake laughed.

"And for your information, if I was in the market for a booty call, which I'm not, I sure as hell wouldn't choose a man who looked exactly like my dead husband."

"You're missing out, Grace. Me and my gun are very popular with the ladies."

I wasn't sure if he was referring to his actual gun or if it was a euphemism. Jake carried a gun when he worked for the FBI and he'd liked it so much that he bought one of his own when he left the bureau a few years ago. I was surprised when he'd announced he was leaving. I always thought he liked working for the FBI. But he said he could make more money in the private sector, which I didn't doubt.

"I'm sure they are, but all I want from you is a ride to Target before they close. Are you going to drive me or do I need to call an Uber?"

Jake smirked but he started the engine.

. . .

"WHAT TOOK YOU TWO SO LONG?" Aunt Maddy asked when Jake and I returned. "MJ's already asleep."

I dropped down onto one of her comfy living room chairs. "What's he sleeping in?" I hoped not the same dirty clothes he'd been wearing for days.

"I found him a pair of shorts and a T-shirt in the lost and found box. What'd you buy?" she asked, nodding at the shopping bags Jake had set down at my feet.

"What didn't she buy?" he answered.

I swatted his leg because with me sitting and him standing that's all I could reach. Most of the awkwardness between us had dissipated as we shopped, but I wanted to stamp out the last bit. "If you had seen their apartment, you'd understand."

"They have a mother, Grace," Jake said.

I looked up at him. "I'm not so sure about that. Or if they have one, she's never around."

"Then call Child Protective Services," he said.

"CPS is not the panacea you think it is." I'd taken on pro bono work for a non-profit children's agency when I'd worked at the law firm in LA. The firm encouraged all its young associates to volunteer their time in order to get more hands-on experience and so the firm could tout their good works in the community. I'd only handled a few cases for the agency, but it didn't take me long to realize that the kids who had been removed from their homes and placed in foster care weren't much better off than the ones who still lived with their crappy parents. Despite that, if I'd seen evidence of abuse, I would've called CPS. And the pediatrician had given Sofia a thorough exam. If she'd seen signs of abuse, she would've called them herself. To me, it just looked like MJ and Sofia were being neglected.

"You can't just keep them," Jake said. "They're not strays."

"I know that. But I can give them food and a place to sleep until I figure out what's going on."

"Until you figure out what's going on?" he said, his voice rising. "Grace, what the hell are you doing? You don't even know these kids."

"Shush," Aunt Maddy said. "They're sleeping. Don't wake them."

"Now you have to know someone to help them?" I said to Jake, keeping my voice low. "What happened to just being a decent human being? They're kids for god's sake."

"Or scammers who pegged you as an easy mark." He huffed.

I jumped up from my chair and faced him. "You did not just say that to me."

Jake stared at me, hands on hips. "I sure as hell did. You have no idea what you're getting yourself into."

"And you do? You've never even had a kid."

"I know enough to know that when you find abandoned kids you call CPS. You don't bring them back to your house and buy them a new wardrobe." Then he pulled his keys out of his pants pocket and stormed out of the house.

Aunt Maddy followed him out to the driveway, and I heard her try to convince him to spend the night and drive home in the morning, or at least stay for coffee and dessert, but Jake refused. After he squealed out of the driveway, Aunt Maddy returned.

"What on earth is going on with you two?" she asked.

"Nothing," I said.

"Don't tell me nothing. Obviously, something."

I had no intention of telling her about our almost crossover from friends to lovers and back again, so I said, "Clearly he doesn't approve of me bringing MJ and Sofia here."

"Well, he does have a point, Grace. You really don't know anything about these kids."

"Seriously? You too?" Jake's reaction wasn't entirely surprising. He and I were on opposite sides of the political spectrum. But Aunt Maddy and I were on the same side.

Aunt Maddy's voice softened. "Sweetie, your heart's in the right place, but you're very vulnerable right now. You're not thinking clearly."

Yes, I'd acted on instinct. But that didn't mean my instincts were wrong. "I had to do something. If you had seen the way they were living, you'd understand. Besides, it's too late to call anyone tonight."

"So you'll call in the morning?" she asked.

I sighed and dropped back down into the comfy chair. "Don't you think we should try to figure out what's going on first? If we call CPS, they'll just come and take them and who knows what'll happen to them."

Aunt Maddy sat down in the chair across from me and leaned in. "Think about what you're doing. You don't know where their mother is. You don't know where their father is, or if they even have a father. You don't know anything about them. There could be drug or alcohol abuse, physical abuse, or god knows what else."

"All the more reason to investigate."

"Grace, it is not your job to investigate!"

"Well, maybe it should be."

Chapter 21

Aunt Maddy offered to watch Sofia while I drove MJ to school the next morning, and I gratefully accepted. I thought perhaps MJ felt like we'd been ganging up on him last night with all the questions and, if I got him alone, he might open up to me.

I thought wrong.

I tried several times to ask him about his mother but I received either one-word answers or no reply at all. At least when I asked him about his father I got a response—he'd died when MJ was seven. He'd been in the Army and was killed in Afghanistan.

MJ needed his backpack for school so we drove to his apartment first. I pulled into the first open parking space I spotted. Unlike in my neighborhood where everyone parked in their own driveway and there weren't many cars on the street, in MJ's neighborhood both sides of the street were filled with parked cars, mostly older-models, although we'd passed one shiny new black BMW. MJ had noticed it too. "Uh-oh," he said.

"Uh-oh?" I asked. But MJ had already jumped out of the car. I shut off the engine and jumped out too. "Wait up."

He glanced back at me but kept walking. "You don't need to come. I'll grab my books and be right back."

"I want to come," I said, as I hurried to catch up to him.

He picked up his speed. "Just wait in the car, okay?"

"No, not okay."

He finally stopped walking and turned around. "Why? You already seen my place."

"I want to talk to your mother. She should be home from work by now, right?" I was willing to play along with the *my-mother-is-at-work* ruse until he told me the truth.

"She's not," he said and turned around, resuming his quick pace.

I followed. "How do you know? You've been with me since yesterday afternoon."

"I just know, okay," he called back to me, not slowing down.

"MJ, I *need* to know where your mother is. That's the only way I can help you."

He stopped again, this time in front of the black, iron gate to his building, which was still propped open with a rock. "My mother's not like you. She don't care what happens to me and Sofia."

This kid was breaking my heart. "That can't be true, MJ. She's your mother. She loves you. Maybe she's just needs a little help too."

"You don't know anything," he yelled and ran for the staircase.

He was right. I didn't. But I was desperate to help him and Sofia, even though it made no sense, not even to me. Maybe it had something to do with Amelia. I couldn't save her. But I could save MJ and Sofia. Or maybe the person I was really trying to save was myself.

Chapter 22

I DIDN'T STOP to think about it. I ran after MJ and caught up with him at the top of the staircase. The only reason I was able to catch him was because a man was blocking his way.

"Yo, MJ, where you been?" the man asked.

"Move," MJ cried and pushed past him. He ran into his apartment and slammed the door shut so hard the front window rattled. It had to have disturbed the neighbors but, surprisingly, no one came out to investigate.

The man, dressed all in black—jeans, leather jacket, hi-top sneakers, even the tattoo peeking out from the top of his black T-shirt was black—stared down at me. "Who are you?" he demanded.

"A friend of MJ's."

His eyebrows shot up and a smile started to form on his lips, but he shut it down. "A friend, eh?"

"And you are?" I asked.

"MJ's uncle. Alex Perez."

"Grace Hughes."

I waited in silence while Alex Perez scanned me from top to

bottom and back up again. "So how did you and my nephew meet?" he asked.

The door to MJ's apartment cracked open and his disembodied voice said, "Grace is a lawyer. She's going to teach me to be a lawyer too."

Alex folded his arms across his chest and shifted his dark-eyed gaze from MJ's front door back to me. "Is that so?"

"Not exactly. But I am a lawyer and MJ is going to start working for me. But at the moment, he needs to get to school. Right, MJ?" I called out.

The front door opened the rest of the way and MJ appeared with his backpack strapped to his shoulders. He pulled the apartment door shut behind him and tried to slip past his uncle, but as he passed, Alex clamped his hand around the back of MJ's neck.

"Not so fast, dawg. Where your mom at?"

Apparently, bad grammar ran in the family. But in Alex's case, I wondered if it was an affectation. Part of the gangster image, along with the all-black clothing and the tattoos.

MJ shrugged. "Don't know. Haven't seen her in a while."

"Why didn't you call me?" Alex asked.

MJ shrugged again.

"I told you, whenever your mom disappears, you call me. *Comprende?*" He reached into his front pocket and pulled out a wad of bills folded in half and held together with a rubber band. He peeled off a bunch of twenties and held them out to MJ, who stuffed them into his back pocket. "Buy some food and clean up the place. It smells like something died in there."

"'K, Uncle A," MJ said, then ran down the steps and out to the street.

Alex turned to me. "You taking him to school?"

"Yes," I said as MJ headed in the direction of my SUV. "Unless you want to."

He shook his head. "Nah, I was never much for school. Dropped out in eleventh grade."

I nodded because I didn't know how else to respond. After an awkward silence, I said, "Well, I should go." But when I turned to leave, Alex placed his hand on my forearm, pinning me, or at least my arm, to the banister. I was taken aback, both at the invasion of my personal space and the unexpected jolt of excitement that shot through me.

"You and me should talk."

I wriggled my forearm out of his grasp and crossed my arms over my chest. "There's a Starbucks on the corner of Main and Second. I could meet you there after I drop MJ at school." I wanted to talk to him too. I thought I might have more luck getting information out of him than MJ. But I preferred to do so in a more populated location. Despite the early hour, or maybe because of it, we were the only two people outside.

Alex smiled as if my suggestion was amusing. "Sure, Starbucks. But give me an hour. I have some business to attend to first."

He didn't offer any information about his business and I didn't ask. I remembered Mike's comment about MJ having an uncle who was a bigtime drug dealer in LA and I wondered if it was true, and if so, if he was referring to Alex.

WHEN I ARRIVED at Starbucks fifty minutes later, Alex was already seated at a table. As I approached his table, he stood up.

"You're early," I said, glancing at my watch.

"My meeting was quick. What can I get you?"

"I can get it."

"No, you're my guest."

I was? I thought I'd invited him. But I wasn't going to argue the point. "Tall latte. Thanks."

He wrapped his knuckles on the table. "Coming right up."

I sat down and stared at my phone to give myself something to do. There was a time when I always had a text message or an email I needed to respond to. But that was Before. No one was ever looking for me in After.

Alex returned to the table with two tall cups. "Bad news?" he asked.

"No," I said, clicking off my phone. I wasn't about to explain to him that I'd been looking at photos of my dead husband and daughter while I waited. My mother had begged me to delete them from my phone—they were all saved on my computer and in the cloud too—but I refused. I was never without my phone so never without pictures of Jonah and Amelia, and I didn't want that to change. "I'll be right back," I said and started to stand up.

"What do you need?" he asked.

"Sugar."

"I'll get it," he replied and was gone before I could object.

The gentleman drug dealer. I admonished myself for making that assumption just because of the way he looked. MJ could have more than one uncle. I had no idea what line of work Alex was in. He could be a brain surgeon for all I knew. Except that he told me he'd dropped out of high school, which eliminated any profession that required a degree. Sales, maybe? But selling what? Just because he drove an expensive car and carried a large wad of cash didn't necessarily mean he was doing something illegal. At best, it was circumstantial evidence. Of course, as every lawyer knew, most cases were built on circumstantial evidence.

Alex returned with an assortment of pastel-hued packets and a wooden stirrer. He set them all on the small table and sat down across from me. He wrapped both his hands around his coffee, but he didn't drink. "So you're a lawyer? For real?"

"Yes," I replied, as I pried the lid off my cup and stirred in two packets of sugar. "Why is that surprising?"

"It's only that you don't look like a lawyer."

I rolled my eyes. "Why? Because I'm a woman?"

"No, the way you're dressed."

He had a point. I never wore yoga pants to the office when I worked at other people's law firms, not even on casual Friday. But I'd lost so much weight that my clingy yoga pants were the only ones that didn't fall down on me, and even these were a lot looser than they used to be.

"I took the day off," I replied then took a sip of my coffee.

"In the middle of the week? What kind of lawyer are you?"

I needed to steer this conversation back to MJ. "So you're MJ's uncle. On his mother's side?" I assumed so since he and MJ had different last names.

"Yes," he replied. "Do you know where she is?"

"No, I was hoping you did."

He shook his head and sighed. "She does this. Disappears for a while. Sometimes a few days, sometimes longer. She always turns up eventually and promises it'll never happen again. But you can't trust an addict, right?"

"Right." I had no idea. We didn't have any addicts in my family, or none that I knew of. "So what happens to MJ and Sofia when she disappears?"

He shrugged. "Depends. Before my mom passed, she used to take care of them. The last couple of times they landed in foster care. From the looks of the apartment, MJ's been trying to do it alone." Almost as an afterthought, he asked, "Where's Sofia? She with you?"

"My aunt. Sofia's sick—nothing serious." I added, although he didn't appear concerned. "She had a fever yesterday, so I took her to the doctor then brought them both back to my aunt's house."

"Why?"

"Well, I wasn't going to bring them back to their apartment. You've seen the place."

"No, I meant, why are you doing this? Who are you to them? For real."

For real, I had no idea.

Chapter 23

"I'm MJ's boss," I said. "Sort of."

Alex leaned back in his chair and folded his arms across his chest. He gazed at me with his intense stare until the oppressive silence wore me down and I confessed everything. Well, not *everything*. Only how I met MJ and Sofia.

"So is this something you do?" he asked. "Take care of kids you don't know?"

"Not usually. This is a first for me."

"Huh." He nodded and sipped his coffee. "So what are you going to do?"

"What do you mean?"

"Are you going to call someone? CPS? If you do, they'll just stick 'em in foster care."

"I don't understand why they have to go foster care. You're a relative. Why can't they just live with you?"

He stared down at the table. When he looked up again he said, "I don't think the social workers consider me a person of good moral character." He didn't use air quotes, but he might as well have. It was obviously a direct quote.

I assumed lacking good moral character was a euphemism

for criminal record and I decided not to ask. "Don't they have any other relatives they could stay with? Another aunt or uncle or grandparent?"

He shook his head. "It's just me and Maria."

"What about on their father's side?"

"Different fathers. MJ's dad was in the Army. He was on his third deployment when his luck ran out. That's when my sister started using. We don't know who Sofia's father is. My sister claims not to know."

"You don't believe her?"

He shrugged. "Could be true. After I cut her off, she would've slept with anyone to get high."

So that answers the *is he or isn't he a drug dealer* question. "Why'd you cut her off?"

"She's my sister," he said, as if the answer should've been obvious.

I took another sip of my coffee and fingered a scratch in the wood table. I had no idea what to say next so I said nothing.

"You got no right to judge me."

"I'm not judging you," I lied. "I don't care what you do for a living." Another lie. "All I really care about is what happens to MJ and Sofia." That part was true.

"Well, that's up to you, counselor."

"How's it up to me? They're *your* niece and nephew."

"You're in it now too, right up to that sweet, tight ass of yours. So what are you gonna do?"

I knew what I should do—what Aunt Maddy and Jake had both urged me to do, call Child Protective Services. That's what the rules called for and Old Grace was a rule-follower. But New Grace had a reckless streak.

Although, was it reckless to not want MJ and Sofia to end up in foster care? I knew some foster parents, maybe even most foster parents, were kind-hearted people who only wanted to help kids in need. But when I'd worked for the non-profit agency I'd been exposed to the other kind of foster parents too, the ones who did it for the money, or worse, abused the kids in their care.

I also knew because of my recent suicide attempt that CPS would never allow the kids to stay with me. At the moment, the State of California didn't even trust me to look after myself; there was no way they'd entrust me with the care of two children. Too much liability. I had no idea what to do.

I set down my coffee and leaned in. "I'm open to suggestions."

"They could live with you," Alex replied, as if it was the obvious answer. "MJ seems real fond of you—and he could do a lot worse than living with the likes of you." He gave me a long eye sweep in case I missed the double entendre.

"Stop it."

"Stop what?"

"You know what."

"Sorry, counselor. I'm just a dumb high school dropout."

He may be a high school dropout, but he wasn't dumb. He knew exactly what he was doing. "Then I'll spell it out for you. No more comments, no more looks, no more touching. If you want me to help your niece and nephew, we need to keep this relationship professional. Understand?"

He shot me another knowing smile and I thought he was going to remark about my characterization of this as a relationship—I'd left myself wide open with that one—but he sat up straight in his chair and said, "Okay. What do you need? Money?" He was already reaching into the pocket of his jeans.

"No, I have money."

He ignored me and pulled out his wad of cash. "How much?"

The woman at the table across from ours, who I was almost

positive was listening to our conversation even though she had her laptop open and earbuds in her ears, openly stared at the bills he was stacking on the table. I smiled at her before I turned back to Alex. I lowered my voice and said, "I told you, I don't want your money. Please put it away." I slid my eyes to the woman across from us.

Alex followed my gaze, then grabbed the bills and stuffed them back into his pocket. "No money. What then?"

"I'm not sure. We need to figure out how to do this so no one gets in trouble."

"You mean so *you* don't get in trouble."

"Yes, Alex, I'd like to not be disbarred if that's okay with you. We need to be smart about this."

"Well, you're the smart one."

I rolled my eyes. "Please. You're plenty smart."

Alex preened as if no one had ever told him that before, which surprised me. It was obvious he was intelligent, just like it was with MJ, bad grammar aside. "Okay, counselor, tell me what to do."

I had the feeling this wasn't the first time he'd uttered those words.

Chapter 24

"What's changed?" Dr. Rubenstein asked when I settled onto her tufted green sofa.

"I give up," I said. "What's changed?"

"You look, dare I say, happy?"

I smiled. Then I thought about Jonah and Amelia and the smile disappeared.

"Oh no. What just happened?"

"Nothing, just ...you know."

Dr. Rubenstein nodded. "That's very common, Grace. Everything's fine, then all of a sudden a memory appears out of nowhere and throws you off balance. That's completely normal."

"I know," I said as I reached for a tissue from the box next to me.

"So let's go back to why you looked so happy a moment ago. What happened today that made you smile?"

I filled her in on the last two days, ending with my coffee with Alex.

"He sounds like a colorful fellow."

I laughed. "That's one way to describe him. Although not in the literal sense since his entire wardrobe is black."

Her eyebrows raised. "His entire wardrobe? You've already had a peek in his closet?"

"No, I don't even know where he lives. And I doubt I'll ever find out."

"Why? It seems like you two hit it off."

"Uh, because he's a drug dealer. Possibly. And definitely a bad boy."

Dr. Rubenstein smiled. "And you don't like bad boys?"

I laughed. "I'm the girl who married the boring accountant, remember?"

"Boring?"

"No, not boring. Jonah was stable and predictable, which is exactly what I like. I save my bad boy crushes for the movies. Have you ever seen Robert Downey, Jr. in *Iron Man*? He's the only bad boy I've ever wanted to sleep with and the odds of that happening are exactly zero."

Dr. Rubenstein laughed. "I agree with you about Robert Downey Jr. I wouldn't kick him out of my bed either. But if real-life bad boys turn you off, then how do you explain that jolt when Alex touched you?"

"I was surprised?"

Dr. Rubenstein shook her head. "No, it was more than that."

"Are you seriously suggesting I date a drug dealer?"

"No, that is not what I'm suggesting at all. I just want you to acknowledge your *feelings*."

"You think I have feelings for Alex?"

"What I think is that you met a man you found physically attractive—even if he's not your usual type," she quickly added. "And that man placed his hand on your body, perhaps innocently, perhaps not, and it caused something inside you to stir.

That is not a bad thing, Grace. It's actually a very good thing. It means you're alive."

"But Jonah's not. And he never will be. And neither will Amelia."

"That's true. But Alex is alive, and so is MJ, and so is Sofia. And so are you, Grace. You're alive, and I want you to stay alive. Do you want to stay alive?"

I nodded. I wouldn't describe myself as happy, but I wasn't feeling suicidal anymore, at least not today.

"Good. What are you feeling at this moment? Don't over-think it. Just tell me the first word that pops into your head."

I closed my eyes and said, "Needed."

"How so?"

I opened my eyes and looked at Dr. Rubenstein. "MJ and Sofia need me."

"We have systems in place for kids in need. Whole depart-ments of people whose job it is to keep kids safe."

I rolled my eyes. "Yeah, we all know how well those work. Those kids need me, and I need them."

"They're not yours, Grace. Taking a child away from a neglectful parent, even an abusive parent, is a Herculean task. Are you sure you want to take that on?"

"It's not what I want to do, it's what I have to do. It's as if the decision's already been made." By God, by fate, by the universe, I couldn't say. It made no sense, not even to me. Yet I couldn't walk away. I just hoped I wasn't going to end up in jail because of it.

Chapter 25

AFTER MY APPOINTMENT with Dr. Rubenstein, I drove to my office and researched child welfare law. I discovered I did not fall into the category of a mandatory reporter—a person, such as a school teacher or police officer, who is required by law to report suspected child abuse or neglect—which was a relief. I would not be breaking the law if I didn't report the situation to Child Protective Services. But lawyers have ethical obligations in addition to legal ones, so I called Alex.

"Yo," he answered.

I laughed. "Most people answer the phone with a hello."

"I'm not most people. What do you need, counselor?"

"To talk to you. Can you stop by my office?"

"No can do. I'm headed back to LA. But I got plenty of juice on my phone."

"That's fine, but I'm going to need you to sign some documents."

"What kind of documents?"

"A retainer agreement. I need you to hire me."

"I already got a lawyer."

"I'm not asking to be your defense attorney. I need you to

retain me so all our conversations about MJ and Sofia are covered by attorney-client privilege. Give me your email address and I'll send you the agreement."

"I'll be there in an hour."

He arrived in forty minutes. It was enough time for me to draft a standard retainer agreement. MJ strode in while his uncle was signing the papers.

"Hey, Uncle A. What are you doing here?"

"I'm hiring your boss to do some work for me."

"Cool," MJ said. "Can I help?"

They both turned to face me.

"Sure, but right now I need you to go out and get me some lunch. I haven't eaten all day. You hungry?"

"I'm always hungry."

Alex and I both laughed. Before I could pull my wallet out of my purse Alex handed MJ a couple of twenties. "Go grab us some subs from that place on California Street."

"They deliver," MJ said. "You want me to call?"

"No," Alex replied. "I want you to *go*. I need to talk to my lawyer. In private."

"Oh, man," MJ said, but he turned to leave.

"Veggie for me," I called out to him. I waited until I heard the front door close before I continued my conversation with Alex. "You need to hire a private investigator."

"Why? Who am I investigating?"

"We need to find your sister."

"I told you. She'll turn up eventually. She always does."

"And I told you, I want this all to be legal. Whatever we do for MJ and Sofia, she needs to sign off. She's their custodial parent. Legally, all I can do without her permission is call CPS, and that is exactly what I *don't* want to do."

Alex sighed but nodded his assent. "I know a guy who's

good at finding people who don't want to be found. But it could take a while. In the meantime..."

"In the meantime, I will look after them and hope that no one who is a mandatory reporter calls CPS and turns us all in."

"I don't think you need to worry."

"That's comforting. Why?"

"You think anybody cares what happens to two poor, brown kids?"

"I'm sure MJ's teachers care." They were legally required to; they were mandatory reporters.

"MJ's been dealing with this shit a long time. He's good at hiding."

That I believed. I considered the implications of this next question but decided I had to ask. "Have you ever thought about having them all move in with you? I don't mean just Sofia and MJ, but their mom too. If all three of them lived with you, CPS wouldn't be involved."

"We tried once. It didn't work out."

I waited for an explanation, but none was forthcoming. I knew I needed to tread lightly, but I couldn't ignore the obvious. "Because of what you do for a living?"

Alex smirked. "What is it that you think I do for a living, counselor?"

"I'm your lawyer now, Alejandro," I said glancing down at the retainer agreement, which contained his full legal name, Alejandro Raphael Perez. "That means our conversations are subject to attorney-client privilege. You can tell me almost anything, and I couldn't disclose that information even if I wanted to."

"*Almost* anything?" His voice was so seductive I felt like he was flirting, or maybe I just wanted him to.

I looked down and focused on straightening the papers on

my desk. "No privilege is absolute. There are always exceptions. But what I'm asking you would fall within it."

He paused then said, "I think we both have some personal business we'd rather not discuss."

I wasn't sure how much he knew about me and how much would turn up in a Google search. "My personal business doesn't involve any illegal behavior." I thought about Jonah's and Amelia's murderer. "At least, not my own illegal behavior."

"Good," he said. "I like my lawyers to be law-abiding citizens."

"And I like my clients to be law-abiding citizens too."

Alex laughed. "Good luck getting clients with that requirement."

"I'm not a criminal defense attorney."

"Then what kind of lawyer are you?"

"The kind who wants to help your niece and nephew."

THE THREE OF us ate our subs together. When we finished, Alex handed MJ a cell phone and told him to call if he needed anything and that he should listen to me.

"No joke, *mijo*," Alex said. "I'm gonna be keeping tabs on you through my new lawyer. I better hear only good things."

"I'm always good, Uncle A." It was the same swagger MJ had displayed the first time we'd met. It had been missing the last couple of days, and I was glad to see it back.

Alex gave MJ a back-slapping hug and then he was gone.

When it was just the two of us, MJ looked at me expectantly. "So what do you want me to do?"

"I want you to tell me the truth about your mother."

Chapter 26

I'D HEARD Alex's version of Maria and now I wanted to hear MJ's version to see if they matched. They did, although MJ's version was more forgiving. He never referred to his mother as an addict.

"So when she disappears like this," I said, "how long is she usually gone?"

MJ shrugged. "Dunno."

"Guess. Days? Weeks? Months?"

"Days mostly. Sometimes a couple of weeks."

"And this time? When's the last time you saw her?"

He shrugged again. "I dunno. Last week?"

"Why didn't you call your uncle?"

He stared down at the ground and mumbled, "Phone wasn't working."

I thought back to Mike Murphy telling me MJ's phone had likely been shut off.

"Okay, MJ, here's the deal. I can't let you and Sofia live alone in that apartment until your mother decides to show up again. So you can either live with me or—"

"Live with you."

. . .

I was stunned when we walked into Aunt Maddy's living room. The basket next to the fireplace that had contained assorted throws as recently as this morning was now filled with Legos, the plant in the corner had been replaced with a doll-house, and an entire shelf of the book case was now devoted to Mo Willems and Dr. Seuss.

"What happened?" I asked.

"We got bored watching television," Aunt Maddy said. "So we did a little shopping."

"A little?" There had to be several hundred dollars' worth of toys and books here.

"You're one to talk. How many outfits did you buy last night? I counted seven for Sofia alone, not including the one she's wearing."

"Yes, one for each day of the week, plus an extra just in case."

Aunt Maddy gave me the arched eyebrow.

"Is it my fault little girl clothes are so cute?"

"No," she said. "And I know how much you miss buying them."

That's all it took for thoughts of Amelia to fill my head and reduce me to tears.

"Are you okay?" MJ asked.

"She'll be fine," Aunt Maddy said. "Why don't you play with your sister for a little while." Aunt Maddy led me into the kitchen and we sat together at the table until I calmed down.

"Maybe having them here isn't good for you."

I shook my head. "No, I'm fine. I'll be fine. I'm just having a moment. Dr. Rubenstein says it's completely normal."

"Good. I certainly wouldn't want an abnormal niece." We both laughed and Aunt Maddy said, "Your mother called. She said she tried you on your cell but you didn't pick up. She got worried."

Was she going to assume the worst every time I didn't pick up or return her call immediately? I already knew the answer to that question—yes. But she'd called this afternoon when I was meeting with Alex. "I was working."

"Working? You have a client?"

"Sort of. It's MJ's uncle. I met him at MJ's apartment this morning when we stopped to pick up his backpack."

"If MJ has an uncle in his apartment, shouldn't the kids be living with him?"

"It's complicated."

She sighed. "It always is." She headed to the refrigerator and yanked open the door. "Red or white?"

Aunt Maddy poured herself a generous glass of Pinot Noir. I stuck with water and filled her in on the day's events.

"Let me get this straight," she said. "They're going to live with you until their mother turns up?"

"Or until the private investigator Alex hires finds her. But don't worry, we won't stay here. I'll bring the kids to my house."

"Don't be ridiculous. Of course, you're staying here. I'm not letting you stay alone."

"But I won't be alone. I'll be with MJ and Sofia. Obviously, MJ will be in school during the day and I was thinking of looking into preschools for Sofia. I'm just not sure I can sign her up without her mother's permission. Although I suppose I could tell them I'm her aunt or something. I mean, are they really going to check? Although I might need her immunization record. That could get tricky."

"Grace, listen to yourself. You sound like you're adopting these kids."

"I can't. Not yet anyway. Adoption isn't even an option until we terminate their mother's parental rights."

"Oh my god, Grace. Stop. Just stop."

"Stop what? This is what you all wanted. You all told me I need to move on with my life and I am."

"No one told you to go out and steal someone else's children!"

"I'm not stealing them. They were abandoned. Their mother left."

"*Temporarily*. She'll come back. That's what MJ told you and this Alex character too. Then what?"

"She's a drug addict, an unfit mother. You don't think I can prove I'm a better parent than she'll ever be?"

"Grace, think. You don't know anything about these kids. Look at the way they were living. They could have serious mental health issues. And if Sofia's mother was using when she was pregnant, Sofia could have problems from that too. You have no idea."

"And she could also be completely fine."

"She's a five year old who doesn't know the alphabet. She's not fine."

"You *tested* her?"

"No, I tried to sing the alphabet song with her and she didn't know it."

"So? Not every child knows the alphabet song. They probably teach it in preschool. Another reason I should sign her up."

"Grace, you are getting way out over your skis. You need to stop and really think about what you're doing."

"I spent two hours this morning researching child welfare law."

"Wow, a whole two hours. I guess that makes you an expert."

"Not an expert, but I do have some idea of what the law is."

"Well, maybe it's time to consult an expert. Isn't there anyone from your law school you could call?"

I leaned back in my chair and considered it. "I can only think of one classmate who went into family law and she's a divorce attorney in Beverly Hills. She probably knows less about foster care than I do."

"Maybe not. Don't a lot of celebrities adopt?"

"Only internationally. No one wants the kid down the street. They like to go to exotic locales. It's a status thing."

"But it's a place to start, right? Surely, she must know other lawyers who do this kind of work."

I had to admit it was a good idea.

Chapter 27

THE NEXT MORNING Aunt Maddy again offered to watch Sofia, who was now fever free. I couldn't help but wonder what my mother would think if she saw them together. For all her warnings that I was in over my head, Aunt Maddy was the one who was getting attached, at least to Sofia. It was Aunt Maddy who spent the whole day playing with her yesterday, fed her dinner, gave her a bath, and tucked her into bed. Sofia rarely spoke, but when she did it was either to MJ or Aunt Maddy, never to me.

I dropped off MJ at school and drove to my office where I spent the morning calling family law attorneys. I started with my former classmate, the divorce lawyer. As I'd predicted, she knew nothing about foster care and terminating parental rights, but she transferred me to her colleague who'd handled an adoption for one of the firm's celebrity clients. That woman referred me to an attorney she knew in the San Fernando Valley who used to work for the county, and on and on it continued until three days later I was standing in the Santa Veneta offices of Janelle Maxwell, Esq.

Calling it offices was being generous. It looked more like a storage unit. The banker boxes were stacked five and six high and there was barely enough open floor space for Janelle, who admittedly was not a small woman, to squeeze through to her desk. I had to move a stack of file folders onto the floor so I'd have a place to sit.

"Sorry about the mess," Janelle said. She smiled showing off a mouthful of straight teeth but for the gap between the front top two. "I'm moving offices this weekend."

"Where to?" I asked.

"Not sure yet."

"You're moving in three days and you don't know where you're going?"

She shook her head, but her long braids, intricately coiled into a crown on top of her head, didn't move. "I know. It's ridiculous. I rented a storage unit for the files, hence all the boxes. I have an appointment to look at another office share this afternoon. I've been looking for months, ever since I got the notice they're tearing this place down to build condos. But the rents have skyrocketed. If I paid what these people are asking, I wouldn't have anything left to live on."

"Do you need to stay in this neighborhood? Because I have an office downtown that's pretty reasonable."

Her eyebrows shot up. "Really? All the spaces I looked at downtown were even more expensive than around here."

I smiled. "You must've been looking by the marina. I'm on Rose, south of Pacific."

"I didn't know they had office buildings down there."

"They don't. I'm in a strip mall."

"Oh," she said, and I could see her mentally adjusting all her assumptions about me.

I'd changed out of my yoga pants for this meeting. I was wearing a navy pinstriped pantsuit that I'd purchased a few months before my wedding when I was at my thinnest, until now. For years it had been too tight for me to wear, but now the

119

pants were baggie and I'd had to pin the waist in the back to keep them from slipping down.

"It's not as awful as it sounds. There's a laundromat next door so it smells great."

"Sounds nice," she said, but her expression implied the opposite. She was probably worried if I could afford to pay her bill. "So what can I help you with today, Ms. Hughes?"

"I need information about terminating someone's parental rights. Sarah Tenley recommended you. She said I'd be in good hands."

"How is Sarah? I haven't seen her in ages."

"I have no idea. I've never met her." I explained how I'd started with my law school classmate and worked my way through multiple referrals until I found her.

She leaned back in her chair and it creaked. "What kind of law do you practice?"

I was starting to hate this question. "I'm not really practicing at the moment."

"Oh. Didn't you just tell me you had an office downtown?"

"Yes. It's complicated."

She glanced at her watch. "Well, I've got forty minutes until I need to leave for my appointment. Start anywhere you'd like."

I began with the day I met MJ and ended with my meeting with his Uncle Alex.

"And you have no idea where their mother is?" she asked, making another note on her yellow legal pad.

"None," I said, "but their uncle—"

"The drug dealer?"

"*Alleged* drug dealer. I have no direct knowledge."

"Noted," she said and double underlined something on her pad.

"I asked their uncle to hire a private investigator to find her."

"And do you know who he hired? Someone local?"

"I don't know. All he said was he knew a guy who was good at finding people who didn't want to be found."

Her eyebrows shot up.

"I know, but it's his sister. He's not going to hire someone to hurt his sister."

"You hope," she said, then set her pen and pad on the desk. "You seem like a kind-hearted person, Ms. Hughes, so—"

"Grace. Please call me Grace."

"Okay, Grace. Call me Janelle. Let me give you some advice. You don't want to do this."

"Why? You think I have a bad case?"

"I think you're going to get your heart broken." She put up her hand to stop my anticipated objection. "I've seen this movie before and I know how it ends. Eventually, you'll find the mother or maybe she just shows up on her own. Either way, instead of realizing that her children, who you've been taking caring of for weeks, months, maybe even years, are best off with you, the mother decides she wants to regain custody. And because the State *always* sides with the biological parent, after her stint in jail or rehab or both, they return custody of her children to her, and you're left devastated."

"What if she relapses? Alex said she's done that before. More than once."

"*When* she relapses the kids go back into foster care and the whole cycle begins again."

"How many chances does she get? At what point does the State say enough is enough and they terminate her parental rights?"

"When she turns up dead from an overdose. Sorry to be blunt, but it doesn't matter how many times she disappears, the State won't involuntarily terminate her parental rights. They'll just keep searching for her until they find her and the whole process repeats."

"So what am I supposed to do? Just bail on these kids?"

"No, you can apply to become a foster parent. The county is always looking for foster parents. There'd be some training involved, a home study, and—"

"Forget it. They'll never approve me."

"Sure they would. I know plenty of people—"

"No, Janelle, they won't. I attempted suicide. Recently," I added before she could ask. I knew from my own research that would disqualify me.

"Oh. Well, yes, that would be an obstacle, at least for the immediate future. But you could wait a year then—"

"A year! You think MJ and Sofia can live on their own for a year? You didn't see their apartment."

"No, Grace, these children cannot live on their own. You need to call Child Protective Services. *Today*."

"But they're not on their own; they're with me. And I'm not turning them in."

"You're not turning them in. No one's getting sent to jail. If a relative can't take them, they'll go to foster care. There are many good homes with loving people, just like you."

I shook my head. "No. MJ trusts me. I won't betray him."

Janelle clasped her hands together on top of her desk. "If you refuse to call CPS then I'm not sure what else I can do for you."

"So that's it? You're refusing to help me? Refusing to help MJ and Sofia?"

"I want to help all of you, Grace, but we need to follow the law. You know that as well as I do."

"Fine," I said and reached for my purse. Janelle Maxwell wasn't the only family law attorney in Santa Veneta. I'd call one of those lawyers who advertised on bus benches. They probably wouldn't mind bending the rules for a good cause or, at least, for a client who could make it worth their while. "I assume you take credit cards," I said as I pulled out my Amex.

She waved the card away. "No charge. Consider it a favor for a friend."

I didn't consider Janelle Maxwell a friend. "We don't know each other. I don't even know your friend Sara."

"I know. But I'm sorry I can't give you the answer you want."

"If lawyers waived their fees every time we told a client something they didn't want to hear, we'd all be out of business."

Janelle laughed. "Maybe that's why I can't afford to pay rent. Speaking of," she stood up. "I really do need to leave for my appointment."

"Right," I said and stood up too. I grabbed a post-it note from the pad on her desk and wrote down my address. I'd planned on ordering business cards, but I hadn't gotten around to it yet. "When you change your mind, you can send the bill to my office."

I figured her invoice would show up in a few weeks. I didn't expect to hear from her again the same day.

Chapter 28

I WAS googling local family law attorneys when I heard the bell on the front door to my office tinkle. The previous tenant, the check-kiting accountant, had left the bell behind and I decided I liked it, even if it was unprofessional. I didn't need to get up to see who it was because MJ was sitting in the reception area doing his homework. But I stopped typing so I could hear their conversation. A woman's voice asked, "Is Ms. Hughes in?"

"Yo, Grace," MJ called out from the next room. "Somebody here asking for you."

Being a good receptionist was not an innate skill. I'd need to train MJ. Before today there'd been no need. I grabbed the suit jacket from the back of my desk chair and walked out to the reception area to meet my first potential client.

"Janelle. What are you doing here?"

"Is this a good time?" She held up the post-it note I'd left for her. "I would've called first, but you only left your address."

I couldn't imagine that she'd driven here just to hand-deliver her invoice, so I figured she had good news. I smiled and said, "Come on in. Can I get you anything? Water? Coffee? Iced tea?"

"Iced tea sounds nice," she said and fanned her face. "It's warm out today."

I hadn't noticed the heat, but I was usually cold these days. I ran back to my office and pulled a twenty out of my purse. I handed it to MJ and said, "Go to the store and buy two iced teas and whatever you want for yourself."

"Food too?" MJ asked.

MJ could eat more than anyone I'd ever met—and he was almost as skinny as me. "Sure, if you're hungry."

"Oh, you don't need to go to the trouble," Janelle said.

"It's no trouble," MJ replied before I could. Then he asked which brand and flavor iced tea we both wanted and sprinted out the door.

"So that's the infamous MJ," Janelle said when we were alone again.

"Yes. Let's go to my office."

Janelle glanced around as I lead her into the back room. "I gotta say this is a lot nicer than I thought it'd be."

I laughed. "I know. Strip mall lawyer doesn't sound too enticing. I probably should've thought of that before I signed the lease."

"How long's your lease?" she asked as she sat down in one of my empty guest chairs, setting her briefcase and purse at her feet.

"Six months."

Her eyebrows shot up. "I know, but you should've seen the place before I moved in. There was an actual blood stain on the wall."

She cringed. "And what kind of law do you practice? I don't think you ever told me."

I nodded to my empty desk. "Well, as you can see, I'm not very busy at the moment. But I used to be a litigator at Simpson & Scott in LA."

"Impressive."

"Not really. I was just another drone associate. I spent most of my time on discovery. But when we moved up to Santa Veneta—"

"We?"

"My husband and I."

She glanced at my empty ring finger. "You didn't mention you were married. That could potentially—"

"I'm not. Not anymore."

"Oh."

"Widowed." I knew she was assuming divorced, and I felt obliged to set the record straight.

"I'm sorry to hear that."

I continued with my CV, which only took another thirty seconds as I'd only worked at one law firm in Santa Veneta before I left for maternity leave.

"So what happened at Wallace?" she asked, using the short-hand for Wallace, Wallace & West. "Too hard adjusting to small firm life? Or did you get tired of the old man leering at you?"

I smiled. I only discovered after I'd taken the job that the senior Mr. Wallace was well-known in the Santa Veneta legal community, both for his schmoozing skills and for his adulteress ways. As a happily married woman, a fact I mentioned regularly when I was in his presence, and then an obviously pregnant one, I'd managed to avoid being the object of the senior Mr. Wallace's advances.

"Neither. I left for maternity leave and never went back."

"You have a child? You didn't mention that either."

"Because I don't anymore." I took a deep breath and spit out the words. "My daughter and husband died together." That was the only part of the story that gave me any comfort. At least, Amelia hadn't died alone.

I was sure if Janelle could have reached my hand she

would've grabbed it, but my hands were folded in my lap. So she had to settle for placing her large ring-free hand on my desk. "I'm very sorry to hear that, Grace."

The tears hadn't leaked out yet, but I could feel them pooling in my eyes and I grabbed a tissue from the box next to my phone.

Janelle leaned in. "May I ask how?"

I nodded as the tears slipped out. "Random shooting on the street. Happened half a mile from the house in broad daylight."

"I remember that story. It was last year in The Hills, right?"

I nodded and blew my nose.

"Didn't the gunman die in a shootout with the police?"

I nodded again. "Yes."

"Well, at least, you were spared a trial."

She was not the first to make that comment. And like the other times I'd heard it, it made me angry. If they'd caught the shooter alive, I might've learned *why* he did what he did. I knew it wouldn't have brought Jonah and Amelia back, nothing could, but maybe it would've given me a sense of closure. But everyone, including Dr. Rubenstein, told me it wouldn't have helped. Still, I wondered ...

I heard the front door tinkle and seconds later MJ barged into my office with our iced teas. I welcomed the interruption. It was an opportunity to change the subject. Although I would've preferred he knocked first.

I waited for MJ to shut the door behind him before I asked Janelle, "So why are you here? Did you change your mind about my case?"

"No. Terminating a biological parent's rights is next to impossible no matter how awful that parent's behavior. I know it's not right, but that's the way the system works. But I felt bad about how we left things and I wanted to tell you if you still wanted my help I'd help you in any way I could."

"Thanks," I said, although if she was still refusing to help me terminate MJ's mother's parental rights, I didn't see what assistance she could provide.

"But now that I'm here, I think I have a better idea."

"Oh?"

Janelle leaned back and smiled. "How would you like to work for me?"

Chapter 29

I couldn't help myself. I laughed.

Janelle folded her arms across her ample chest. "You find job offers funny?"

"Sorry," I said, since it was clear she was insulted. "It's just that those were the last words I expected to come out of your mouth."

"Why? You're a lawyer and I'm a lawyer. It happens all the time."

"Because I have zero family law experience. I just tried to hire *you* a few hours ago because I have no idea what I'm doing. Now you want to hire me?"

"Alright," she said, unfolding her arms. "I can see where my offer might come as a surprise. But I think with your background, this could work."

"My background?"

"You're a litigator so you already know the basics. The rest I can teach you."

"Surely you can find another lawyer with litigation experience."

"Yes, I had a young woman working for me for several years.

She left just last week. I think the prospect of us not having an office scared her. And Cadawaler Erickson offered her more than I can afford to pay."

"They're divorce lawyers, right?" Their name came up when I was googling local family law attorneys.

"Yes, and they have a small estate planning practice too."

"I assume that means their clients are on the higher end of the income scale." Only people with significant assets hired estate planning attorneys.

"Yes, and that's where you come in. Did you know that in divorce cases with contentious custody disputes, the courts will sometimes appoint separate counsel for the child?

"No. I told you, I know nothing about family law."

"The court appoints the counsel, but it's the parents who split the bill.

"So no one's happy."

"Exactly. The pay's not great. It'll be less than you made at Simpson & Scott. Maybe less than you made at Wallace too. But the work can be very rewarding. Since you're a neutral third party acting in the best interests of the child, your recommendations carry a lot of weight with the court."

I sat up straighter. "Okay, I'm listening." Even though I'd enjoyed the pro bono cases I'd worked on when I was at Simpson & Scott, I'd never considered making that my career. The pay would've been way too low. But my financial circumstances had changed. "The money's not an issue, but if this is such a great gig, why do you want to hand it off to me?"

"I wouldn't hand *all* of it off to you. But I have more work than I can handle, and frankly there are some parents I'd rather not have to deal with."

"Why? Because they try to get you to side with them instead of their kid so they can screw over their ex?"

She laughed. "They *all* do that. I just think some of them

would be more comfortable dealing with someone like you than someone like me."

"What do you mean someone like me?" When she didn't answer right away I jumped to my own conclusion. I didn't know why I lowered my voice to a whisper, but I did, the same way my mother lowered her voice to a whisper when she told me someone she knew had contracted cancer. "Is it because I'm white?"

"It's more than that," Janelle huffed. "I know a woman in Santa Barbara who does this kind of work. She's Black too, but the rich folks are just fine with her. But she doesn't look like me. She looks like you, only Black. And she went to the fancy law school too," she said, nodding to the framed diploma on the wall behind me.

I understood. I'd worked with several Black and brown lawyers at my firm in Los Angeles. But all my non-white colleagues went to top-tier law schools and dressed in the de rigueur dark suits. And all the Black women straightened their hair. None of them braided their hair or wore brightly colored patterned dresses, at least not to the office.

"Those rich folks treat me like something stuck to the bottom of their shoe," she continued. "Especially when I tell them something they don't want to hear."

"That really sucks, Janelle. I'm sorry you have to deal with that."

She shrugged. "So what do you say? You want to give this a try?"

Chapter 30

"I'M CONFUSED," Aunt Maddy said. "I thought you didn't want to work for anyone else anymore. Isn't that why you started your own firm?"

We were seated at her kitchen table. Normally we chatted in the living room because it was more comfortable, but MJ had commandeered the space since it was the only room in the house with a television. I'd waited to have this conversation with my aunt until after she'd put Sofia to bed, a task I'd offered to do but which my aunt insisted on doing herself. I was sure if Sofia was an infant instead of a five-year-old, my aunt would've already bought a Baby Bjorn and would be wearing her around the house. In just a few days, the two had become inseparable.

"I wouldn't be working *for* Janelle," I said. "Not really."

"You just said she offered you a job."

"She did."

"How is that not working for her?"

Aunt Maddy was a great interrogator, probably from her years of interviewing people. She zeroed in on the slightest inconsistency. "It's more like an apprenticeship. She'll show me the ropes for six months, and if it doesn't work out, we go our separate ways."

"And if does work out?"

"Then we partner. Legally. For now, we'll be working out of the same office, but we'll keep our professional corporations separate."

"So you're moving offices too?"

"No, she is. She's moving into my office. We're going to put up another wall," I offered before she could ask. "We don't need that huge reception area. Janelle says most of the time she meets with clients in their home or at school. And she's at court appearances at least once a week. We need an office, but neither one of us will be spending much time there." I thought that last part would appeal to my aunt, and no doubt my mother, when my aunt relayed this conversation to her.

"Okay," she said.

"Okay?"

"Well, it's not like you're asking my permission."

"No, but I'd still like your opinion."

She stared at me and sighed. "You've become another person, Grace. I hardly recognize you anymore. And I'm not just talking about your hair."

I went for a haircut this morning. But instead of a trim, which had been my intention when I'd walked into the hair salon a few doors down from Starbucks, I asked the hairdresser to cut off half the length and layer what was left. I needed highlights too, since mine had grown out ages ago, but I wasn't willing to trust my color to a new stylist. I'd have to work up my resolve before I returned to my former hair salon in The Hills though. I'd only been back once since Jonah's and Amelia's death, and it had been uncomfortable experience for both of us. I knew it was my fault. I wasn't able to keep up my side of our usual patter about family and friends.

My evolution from Old Grace to New Grace was not yet complete, but the job with Janelle would be a mark of my progress.

Or so I thought.

THE NEXT MORNING after I drove MJ to school, which was now our custom, instead of heading to my office, I returned to the Guest House. I stopped at the bakery first to pick up cinnamon rolls. When I walked into the kitchen, Aunt Maddy was pouring cereal into a bowl for Sofia.

"What's wrong?" Aunt Maddy asked as soon as I appeared in the doorway.

"Nothing," I said, "but hold off on the milk." I set down the bakery box in the center of the table. You could smell the cinnamon and sugar even before I lifted the lid.

Sofia's eyes widened as I placed a gooey cinnamon bun on a plate and slid it in front of her. It was still warm from the bakery's oven.

"Have you ever had one of these before?" I asked.

Sofia shook her head. She rarely spoke to me. I would've been concerned if I thought she *couldn't* speak, but I knew that she could because I often heard her and MJ whispering to each other at night when I walked by their room, and she talked to Aunt Maddy too.

"Try it," I said. "You'll like it."

She turned to Aunt Maddy for approval.

"Go ahead," Aunt Maddy said.

Only then did Sofia take a bite. Judging from the smile on her face, my assumption was correct.

"The other one's for you," I said, placing the second cinnamon roll on a plate and pushing it toward Aunt Maddy's usual seat at the table.

"And what are you going to eat?" she asked.

I held up my to-go coffee cup.

She placed her hand on her hip and stared at me.

I rolled my eyes like a teenager and said, "Oh fine. I'll split it with you."

I nibbled on the cinnamon roll while I waited for Sofia to finish eating. When only a few crumbs were left on her plate, I tried to cajole her into the living room with the promise of a new toy, but she wouldn't budge. It was only after Aunt Maddy knelt down in front of her and said, "I'm right here if you need me," and gave her a fierce hug that Sofia would leave the room.

"Apparently, I'm not the only one who's become another person," I said as I picked at the icing on my half bun.

"You know I've always liked kids. Wasn't I the best aunt ever? That's what you used to tell me when I let you stay up late and watch R-rated movies."

I smiled at the memory. "Yes and you still are."

"Alright, Gracie, what do you want?"

I tried to look innocent, but apparently I failed.

Aunt Maddy held up what was left of her cinnamon roll. "I recognize a bribe when I see one."

"Not a bribe. I just wanted to do something nice for you since you've done so much for me, especially lately."

"Uh huh," she said and popped a wedge of gooey cinnamon and sugar into her mouth. "And feel free to bribe me with these anytime," she added, sucking the icing off her fingers. "So what is it that you want, my darling?"

"It's not just what I want but what you want too."

Aunt Maddy hooted and crossed her arms over her chest. "Oh, this should be good."

"I'm serious. I think it's fair to say that you've become attached to Sofia and would be sad to see her leave, right?"

Aunt Maddy turned serious. "I did warn you this would

happen, Grace."

She warned me it would happen to *me*, not to her. And it hadn't happened to me, at least, not with Sofia. I'd become very attached to MJ and I'd be devastated if someone told me I could never see him again. But whenever I spent time with Sofia, I felt...nothing. Actually, it was worse than nothing; it was almost an aversion. I wasn't merely grateful when Aunt Maddy kept offering to take care of Sofia for me, I was relieved.

This was something I'd discussed with Dr. Rubenstein. I realized that when I was with MJ my thoughts naturally turned to the future. I wanted to help him reach his full potential and fantasized about what he might achieve. I also just enjoyed his company. He made me laugh. But whenever I spent time with Sofia, I was dragged back to the past. Every time I looked at her, I thought about Amelia and what might have been if only...

I knew it wasn't fair of me to feel this way. It wasn't Sofia's fault her mere presence depressed me. She was a sweet little girl, and it was heartening to watch her respond to all the attention Aunt Maddy lavished on her. She was like a flower turning toward the sun. Maybe if I spent more time with her, she would respond that way to me too, but I didn't. And I felt guilty about that. Just not guilty enough to make me change my behavior, apparently.

I took a deep breath and forced myself into the present. "You did warn me. But here we are. And Janelle's convinced me that we need to contact CPS." She'd actually made it a condition to my working with her.

"Well, at least one positive has come out of this Janelle business," Aunt Maddy replied.

I let the subtle dig at my new law partner slide and continued. "I was right to think that no one's going to let me become a foster parent so soon after my suicide attempt. Janelle confirmed it."

"I'm sorry to hear that. But I can't say I'm surprised." Aunt Maddy popped the last bite of cinnamon roll into her mouth and wiped her hands on a napkin.

"Janelle said maybe I could get approved in a year or two, but MJ and Sofia can't wait that long. They need placement now. And Janelle has come up with a solution."

"That's wonderful," Aunt Maddy said, but her tone implied the opposite. "I don't think we want to rush into anything though. I mean, these kids have been through enough. I don't think moving them again so soon is the best idea. Make sure Janelle knows that I have no problem with them staying here as long as they like."

"Thanks, but I think when they make a change, it happens quickly. Janelle mentioned something called an emergency placement."

I could see the panic in my aunt's widened eyes. "But we'd still be able to visit, right? I mean, these kids need continuity in their lives. Surely CPS understands that."

"I don't think it works that way. I think if you leave a home you cut ties. There are no visitation rights that I'm aware of."

"You mean they'll just take them from us and we'll never see them again?"

"Yes, but there is an alternative. We could not give them up."

Aunt Maddy cocked her head to the side like a puppy. "You lost me."

"Janelle said *I'm* not eligible to be a foster parent, but *you* are."

"*Me?*"

I can't take credit for convincing Aunt Maddy; it was the thought of never seeing Sofia again. Aunt Maddy couldn't bear it. So even after I told her that she'd have to take parenting classes, and submit to social worker interviews, and agree to be fingerprinted, and consent to a background check, and endure a home safety assessment, she still agreed.

"But all that must take time," Aunt Maddy said. "What happens to Sofia and MJ in the interim?"

"That's where the emergency placement comes in. Janelle thinks she can get us approved, if their uncle signs off on it. But since you would technically be the foster parent, not me, they would have to live here with you."

"Of course they're going to live here with me. Where else would they live? But MJ needs his own room. I'm not comfortable with him and Sofia sharing." She held up her hands as if physically warding off any argument. "I know they're siblings. But he's a teenage boy, Grace. It's not appropriate."

Aunt Maddy had segued into my next topic for me. Janelle wasn't concerned about MJ and Sofia sharing a room as long as they slept in separate beds, but she was concerned that Aunt Maddy might not get approved if she was still renting out rooms to strangers. She hadn't had any guests since we arrived. But summer was her busiest season and it was only two months away.

"I don't disagree. But if we all have our own rooms,"—I assumed I would be staying here for the foreseeable future too—"there's only one bedroom left. And I assume you'll want to keep that one empty for when Mom comes to visit." My mother could always stay at my house, but I knew she wouldn't want to. She'd want to be where the action was, even if she didn't approve.

"You're right," Aunt Maddy said and pushed back from the table. "I better go cancel the bookings for the summer. Maybe I'll call around first and see who else has openings so I can make recommendations. And I'll put an announcement on the website too."

She was on her way out of the kitchen when I said, "Wait.

We're not done. We still have to figure out the money."

She turned and stared at me. "What money?"

"The money you'll be losing by not renting out rooms. I need to pay you."

"Pay me? Grace, we're family. You don't pay family. Besides, doesn't the State pay foster parents?"

They did, but only *after* you'd been approved for the program, and that could take months. I was sure Alex would offer Aunt Maddy money, but I didn't think she'd want his money any more than I did. "But I want to pay. Room and board for all three of us."

"Don't be ridiculous. I'm not taking your money."

"Then don't think of it as my money. Think of it as the insurance company's money because that's what it is."

"Jonah paid for that policy. It's your money. You should know that; you're the lawyer."

"He took out a five million dollar life insurance policy six months before he died. No matter how high the premium, he didn't pay that much for it."

"That's the nature of insurance. Sometimes the insurance company wins and sometimes you do. You hit the jackpot, Grace."

I winced. I'd gladly give back every penny to get my husband and child back.

"Sorry, sweetie, I didn't mean that the way it sounded. I just meant—"

"I know what you meant. But I *need* you to take this money from me. It's the only way I can do this with a clear conscience. I'm already wrecking your life. I can't wreck your finances too!"

She crossed the kitchen and enveloped me in the same fierce hug she'd given Sofia. She released me and placed her hands on my shoulders. "Listen to me. You haven't wrecked my life. Just the opposite. Do you know why I bought this place?"

"Because you wanted to retire but couldn't afford to?"

She laughed. "Well, yes, that was part of it. But the real reason was that after your Uncle Ben died, I was lonely."

"Why didn't you move up to San Francisco?" My mother had begged her to come.

"You know I love your mother dearly, but if I'd moved to San Francisco, we would've killed each other by now. You know how possessive she can be. She never would've allowed me to have a life of my own. And can you really imagine me playing bridge all day?"

"Then why didn't you move to LA? You know you were always welcome at my house."

"Grace, you were a newlywed. You didn't need your old aunt hanging around."

"But Jonah loved you. He always said you were his favorite of my relatives."

"And I loved him too. But I needed to create a life for myself and I did. I like teaching at the community college, and I like having guests in my home. Nothing will change now, except instead of having strangers staying for a few days, it'll be my favorite niece—"

"I'm your only niece."

"And two good kids who need a home. It's a blessing, Grace."

"Are you sure? Because I feel like this isn't what you had planned for your life. C'mon, did you ever imagine yourself becoming a foster parent at sixty?"

"Fifty-nine," she said. "I've still got two months left. And yes, I'm sure. It's scary how much I've come to care about those kids in such a short amount of time."

I felt exactly the same. And for the first time since Jonah's and Amelia's death, I prayed. I prayed to God that MJ's and Sofia's mother would never come back.

Chapter 31

"I'm worried about you," Dr. Rubenstein said after I'd told her about my new job working with Janelle and my aunt's emergency foster parent application.

"I'm a little worried too," I replied, "but Janelle thinks Aunt Maddy will get approved. She already passed the home inspection and she's getting fingerprinted this afternoon."

Dr. Rubenstein shook her head and her silver earrings caught the early afternoon sunlight, temporarily blinding me. Dr. Rubenstein noticed and she crossed the room to shift the angle of the vertical blinds. "I'm not worried about the emergency placement," she said, returning to her seat. "I'd be surprised if your aunt didn't pass. There's always a shortage of good foster placements, especially ones who are willing to take multiple children on short notice. It's *you* I'm worried about."

"Me? Why?" I was finally feeling like I was making some progress. I was even going to suggest that we cut down my sessions to once per week. "Do you think working with Janelle is a bad idea? I thought it would be a good opportunity for me."

"It's not the job per se I'm concerned about. It's that you

seem entirely focused on getting permanent custody of MJ and his sister, which may or may not happen."

"I know it won't be easy. Maria will turn up eventually."

"And when she does, she'll want her children back. Have you thought about how you'll feel then? You've already lost one child, Grace. Do you really want to lose two more?"

The reference to Amelia, even obliquely, felt like a slap in the face. "You don't *know* she'll want her children back. Maybe she'll see how well they're doing with me and my aunt and she'll decide they're better off. Janelle told me it's easy to adopt if the biological parents agree to terminate their own parental rights. And we'd only need Maria's consent. MJ's dad is dead and no one knows who Sofia's father is, not even Maria."

Dr. Rubenstein took her feet off the ottoman and leaned forward in her chair. "Grace, listen to me," she said, her voice uncharacteristically sharp. "Maybe you'll get to keep MJ and Sofia long-term, maybe you won't. It's impossible to know at this point. But even if you do get to keep them, they are not a substitute for Amelia."

"I know that," I said defensively. I could feel the tears forming in my eyes.

"Good." She leaned back in her chair. "Let's spend some time talking about your loss."

"Why?" I asked, the tears now spilling out and sliding down my cheeks. "It's not going to bring them back."

"I know you'd like nothing more than to skip over the grieving part and move on to something new. It's what you've been doing for the last sixteen months. But it won't work. The only way out of the pain is through it."

The only way out of the pain is through it. It was her mantra lately, and I was sick of hearing it. "But I can't go through it," I cried. "You know that. Every time I try, I get stuck. Is that what you want? You want to see me back at the Wellstone Center?"

Her voice and expression softened. "Grace, that's not going to happen."

"You don't know that!"

"I do know that because I know you. You're stronger than you think you are. And I promise you that you will get through this. You just have to try."

I loudly sniffed back my tears. "You mean someday I'll wake up and not miss them so much my whole body aches?"

"You'll always miss them, Grace. You will never not feel that loss. But you will heal."

I snorted. Healing sounded like a fantasy. One of those woo-woo Instagram memes with a woman in yoga pants standing on top of a mountain staring off into the distance. I lived in the real world where the only way to move on was to actually *move on.* New job, new life, new everything. But Dr. Rubenstein made me promise that before our next session I'd go back to my house and "sit with my grief."

I would go back to my house, as promised, but I had no intention of sitting with my grief. I did, however, need to pick up my mail and grab my work clothes.

I ALLOWED my anger to fester while I drove from Dr. Rubenstein's office to my house in The Hills. Sit with my grief? What the hell good would that do? It wouldn't bring Jonah and Amelia back, it would just depress me. Wasn't the point of therapy to make you less depressed, not more? Maybe I needed to find a new therapist.

But my anger gave way to shock when I saw my dead husband's car parked in my driveway.

Chapter 32

I PULLED into the space next to the Audi and walked to my front door on wobbly legs. I knew Jonah wasn't home. Obviously. I wasn't experiencing a psychotic break. But seeing his car parked in the driveway still shook me.

I had my key in my hand, but before I placed it in the lock, I turned the knob on the front door. It opened and I walked in.

"Hello?" I called out to the empty first floor.

Not surprisingly, the ghost of my dead husband did not respond. But that didn't stop my heart from racing. Then I looked up and spotted the ghost of my dead husband at the top of the staircase.

I didn't faint. I just allowed myself to collapse onto the floor and close my eyes. It was Jake's voice, his insistent, "Grace, are you okay?" that forced me to open them again. I knew I was staring up into Jake's face, not Jonah's, but they were so similar...

"Do you want some water?" he asked. "Wait here. I'll get you some water."

By the time Jake returned with a glass of water, I'd recovered the power of speech. "What are you doing here? You scared the living daylights out of me."

"Nice to see you too," Jake said.

He handed me the glass and I took a sip of the cool water. I set the glass on the console table and pulled myself up. "I'm serious. You nearly gave me a heart attack. How did you get in here?"

Jake pulled a silver key out of the front pocket of his jeans. It matched the key still gripped in my hand.

"Where did you get a key to my house?"

"Jonah," he said as if it was obvious. "He gave it to me when you two moved in."

"No, he didn't." Jonah and I had discussed this. We agreed that in case of an emergency, someone should have a spare key to our house, but we decided that someone should be my aunt since she lived the closest.

"He did," Jake insisted.

He had to be lying. Jonah would've told me if he'd given Jake a key. It's something we would've discussed beforehand. "If you've had a key all these years, why have you never used it before?" Whenever Jake visited, he always rang the bell.

"It was for emergencies. I would never just let myself in."

"Well, you let yourself in today. What's the emergency?"

He lowered his head and glanced at me through a heavy fringe of dark eyelashes. No doubt that look had helped him get out of jams with plenty of women in the past, but it wasn't going to work on me.

"Jake, why-are-you-here?" I asked, enunciating each word.

"I'm in town. For work."

"Then why didn't you call me?"

"I didn't think you'd want to see me. The last time at your aunt's house you weren't very friendly."

"*I* wasn't friendly? You're the one who got all mad at me and left in a huff."

"I wasn't mad at you. I just thought you were getting in over

145

your head with those kids, which is the last thing you need right now. What did you end up doing? Did you call CPS?"

"Yes. Eventually. But MJ and Sofia are still living with us. Aunt Maddy's applied to become a foster parent."

"Wow," he said, "I didn't see that one coming."

"Me either. But she's gotten very attached to Sofia, and now she doesn't want to give her up."

"Can she keep her? I thought their mother was still alive."

"She is. It's complicated." But I didn't want to get side-tracked. "You still haven't told me what you're doing here. I mean *in my house*," I added before he could give me the I'm-in-town-for-work line again.

"Oh, that." He shot me the Hughes smile. "I probably should've warned you. I figured since you were staying with your aunt, you wouldn't be here. And judging by the amount of mail I found in your box, you haven't been. It looked like mostly junk, but I didn't want to throw any of it away in case you wanted it. I left it for you in the kitchen."

"Thanks," I said, just now realizing that I'd forgotten to stop at the mailbox on my way in.

"So I should probably leave you to it," he said turning toward the door.

"Wait. You still haven't told me why you're here." And he seemed intent on *not* telling me, which was weird. Did he bring a woman here? Surely, if he was seeing someone locally, he'd go back to her place, wouldn't he?

"Actually, it's a little embarrassing."

"Jesus," I sighed and closed my eyes. "Please tell me you did not just have sex with some random woman in my bed." I suddenly remembered a story Jonah had told me from when he and Jake had lived together in college. He'd walked in on Jake and his latest conquest having sex on the kitchen counter. Or at least the woman was on the kitchen counter. Jake was pushed up against her, naked but for his pants around his ankles. Ugh. Now I was going to have to scrub my entire kitchen with bleach.

He snorted. "No, Grace, I did not bring a woman to your house and have sex with her in your bed. Or any other bed."

"The floor? The couch? The kitchen counter? I hear you're a fan of kitchen counters."

His mouth dropped open, but he quickly recovered. "I can't believe Jonah told you about that."

I chuckled. "Jake, you know Jonah and I didn't keep secrets from each other."

He stared at me so long I was about to ask him if he thought spouses *should* keep secrets from one another, when he glanced down at his watch.

"Oh shit, I didn't realize it was so late. Gotta go." He leaned in and kissed me on the cheek. "Raincheck on dinner. But definitely next time I'm in town."

A few seconds later I heard the Audi's engine rumble and the tires screech as he backed out of the driveway. And he was gone.

That was just weird, I thought as I brought the glass of water into the kitchen and set it down in the sink. It didn't look like anyone had been having sex on the countertop. The coffeemaker, toaster oven, and spice rack were all in their usual place. But I still sprayed down the counters with disinfectant just to be safe.

After flipping through the mail, mostly junk as Jake had said, I took a deep breath and headed toward the staircase. When I reached the second floor landing, I instinctively turned towards Amelia's room then quickly turned around. There would be no sitting with my grief today.

I headed into the master bedroom, which was still in the same state it had been the last time I was here—windows open and bed stripped bare. Whatever Jonah was doing in my house today must not have involved my bed because he would've at least put a sheet on it.

I closed the bedroom windows and headed into the walk-in closet. All my work clothes were still hanging on the right side in a color-coded row. Now that I was working again, I couldn't just wear yoga pants every day. I fingered the arms of the suit jackets. I could probably still wear them even if they were a little loose, but the pants would all have to be taken in. The shirts and shoes would still fit though.

I grabbed my suitcase from the top shelf and started tossing in pantsuits and silk shirts. Then I turned to Jonah's side of the closet. My chest tightened as I stared at his neat row of dress shirts, mostly white with a few light blue. All his clothes were still there except for one pair of shoes and the black suit, white shirt, and gray tie we'd buried him in. I reached for the navy sweater I bought him our last Christmas together. It was the softest cashmere I'd ever felt, and as soon as my hand swept over it in Nordstrom's, I knew I'd buy it, despite it costing way more money than I'd ever spent on a sweater before.

I loved the color on Jonah, how the dark blue fabric highlighted his bright blue eyes and how I could see a hint of chest hair peeking out from the high V-neck. The sweater was so soft that whenever he wore it, I was constantly touching him—his arms, his back, his chest—which quickly made the sweater Jonah's favorite too. He knew the odds of getting sex from me increased exponentially on nights he wore that sweater.

When Jonah first died, I used to wear the sweater all the time. I'd bury my nose in the fabric and breathe in his scent. But his scent faded from it long ago, and at some point, someone, probably my mother, had sent the sweater to the cleaners and now it just smelled like dry cleaning fluid.

I refolded the sweater and placed it back on the shelf. My mother was right. I needed to donate Jonah's clothes. But that would require going through them and boxing them up, and I was not yet ready for that task. Soon, maybe, but not today.

I zipped the suitcase closed, pulled out the handle, and wheeled the bag out of the bedroom. I had my hand on the staircase railing when I stopped and glanced back at the doorway to the third bedroom, which had been Jonah's home office/gym before Amelia was born. After Amelia was born, that room became our shared home office, and Jonah's weights were relegated to the garage.

The door to the third bedroom was partially closed, which was odd. I always kept that door fully open. I left my suitcase at the top of the stairs and headed inside.

Chapter 33

THE BEDROOM FELT cluttered with two desks and a sleeper sofa. If I put the house up for sale, I'd have to take out one of the desks.

Put the house up for sale? Where had that come from? It was like I was suddenly channeling my mother. All the things she'd been telling me to do for months, and which I'd steadfastly refused to do, now seemed like possibilities.

It was the door that had caught my attention, but now that I was inside the room, I noticed Jonah's desk chair was out of place. The big, black, faux-leather chair was normally pushed in and facing the desk, but today it was pulled out slightly and the seat was angled toward the door.

"What the heck?" I said to the empty room. I crossed the room to push it back into place, but when I touched the faux-leather arm, it was warm. And the seat was even warmer. It was obvious someone had recently been sitting in the chair, and that someone could only be Jake.

Motherfucker.

I pulled my phone out of my purse and called him. I was going to demand he tell me why he'd been at my house today, but my call went straight to his voicemail and I didn't leave a message.

I sat down in the still-warm chair and studied Jonah's desk. Other than the chair, nothing seemed out of place. The computer screen, keyboard, and empty docking station were all cool to the touch. And the desk lamp, pencil cup, and two photos—one of Jonah and I from our last pre-Amelia beach vacation, and one of Jonah and Amelia taken right after she was born—were gathering dust in their usual spaces.

I pulled open the top desk drawer, which contained post-it notes in various sizes, two boxes of paperclips, and an assortment of pens. If something was missing, would I even know? I'd never rifled through Jonah's desk before. I'd trusted my husband. There was no reason to snoop.

I moved to the middle drawer which held only blank pads of paper and, finally, the bottom drawer, which was meant to hold hanging files but which was currently empty. Did there used to be files in there? I couldn't remember. I knew Jonah had kept files in that drawer when we'd lived in LA, but before we moved to Santa Veneta, he scanned a bunch of documents and shredded the originals.

Was that why Jake was here? Was he looking for something in Jonah's desk? If he was, why not just tell me? I would've offered to help him search. None of this made any sense.

My phone pinged and the calendar reminder popped up on the screen. Shit. I was supposed to meet Janelle at the courthouse in fifteen minutes. My first court appearance in almost two years and I was going to be late.

Chapter 34

THIS WAS my first time inside the downtown Santa Veneta courthouse. The courtrooms looked the same as all the Los Angeles county courtrooms I'd appeared in—linoleum floors, acoustic ceiling tiles, and scarred furniture. When I worked at the law firm in LA, most of my court appearances were in Federal court. Federal courtrooms look like the courtrooms in television shows. They're majestic spaces with dark wood paneled walls, high ceilings, and tall windows. County courtrooms look like the DMV with less Plexiglas but just as much waiting.

I found Janelle sitting on the back bench of our assigned courtroom, and I slid into the space next to her. "Sorry I'm late," I whispered.

"No matter," Janelle replied. She nodded to the filled benches in front of us. "It looks like we're going to be here a while."

I listened to Judge Ryan, a balding older white man who wasn't particularly friendly to any of the litigants, as he briskly moved through the cases before him. When the clerk called our case, I followed Janelle up the center aisle and headed left toward the defendant's table, but Janelle walked past it to a third table off to the side.

"Where are we going?" I whispered.

"This is where he likes the minor's counsel to be," she whispered back.

I watched as two other sets of lawyers filled out the plaintiff's and defendant's tables.

The judge read the file for maybe twenty seconds before he looked up. "Motion for continuance?"

"Yes, your honor," Plaintiff's counsel said. "We need more time to—"

"Any objection?" the judge asked Defendant's counsel.

Defendant's counsel stood up, said, "No, your honor," and sat back down.

The judge swiveled to our table. "And you?"

Janelle stood up so I did too. "No, your honor, but I want to notify the court that I have a new partner who—"

"Name?" he asked.

"Grace Keegan Hughes," I replied.

The judge stared at me over the top of his small wire-frame glasses. "I haven't seen you in my courtroom before, Ms. Hughes."

"No, your honor." I knew better than to try to explain anything to him.

"Have you completed the required training?"

"She's in the process," Janelle answered before I could. "I'll be supervising her on this one until she's certified."

"Then I'll leave both your names as counsel of record for the minor. Motion for continuance granted." He rapped his gavel and the clerk called the next case.

Our appearance in front of the judge lasted less than ninety seconds. It would've been less than a minute if Janelle hadn't introduced me.

Janelle followed Plaintiff's counsel and Defendant's counsel down the center aisle and outside the courtroom, so I did too. Janelle introduced me when we reached the hallway and I shook hands with both of them.

Plaintiff's counsel, a middle-aged man in an expensive suit, checked his equally expensive watch. "I've got another appearance in front of Judge Kell. Nice meeting you." He turned on his heel and headed down the hallway.

Defendant's counsel, who looked a few years older than me and wore a black linen sheath dress with a black blazer over it, pulled a business card out of her giant shoulder bag and handed it to me. "Call me to arrange access to your client."

"You? Not her parents?"

"Trust me, you'd much rather deal with me than her mother. Nice seeing you, Janelle." Then she too disappeared into a sea of people in the crowded hallway.

I turned to Janelle, who pulled a thick legal file out of her wheeled briefcase and dropped it into my outstretched hands. It must've weighed at least five pounds. "She's all yours."

Of course I had questions, but Janelle had another court appearance too. "Read the file," she said. "We'll talk later." Then she returned to the same courtroom we'd just exited to wait for her next case to be called.

WHEN I ARRIVED at the office, MJ was already sitting at his desk playing a game on the phone Alex had given him. "Short day for some teacher thing," he said before I could ask.

"Hungry?" I replied, already knowing the answer. I handed him a twenty and sent him out to buy lunch while I settled in with the thick file.

Fifteen-year-old Olivia Baylor's father had filed for divorce over a year ago and her parents were still fighting over everything, including her custody. Olivia currently lived with her mother in Monteverde, which was within the boundaries of Santa Veneta County, but was really its own isolated world. Monteverde was where the wealthy people lived. Although I doubted anyone who lived in that neighborhood owned just one home.

Olivia was in her freshman year at Winston Academy, an exclusive private school I only knew existed because one of my former mommy friends had an older step-daughter who she and her husband were trying to get accepted there. The couple were well off, but not well off enough to make a six-figure donation to the school. As she'd explained to me, to get accepted to the Winston Academy, you had to have a really smart kid or a ton of money or ideally both.

Olivia's parents definitely had a ton of money, which didn't mean Olivia wasn't a smart kid too. I flipped through the file until I found her school records. Her test scores were high, but her grades were mediocre. Smart kid who didn't work hard because she knew she didn't have to, I concluded. I'd known a few of those kids in college. There were less of them in law school. The rich kids who went to law school were usually ambitious. Law school was just their first step to a job in the DA's office of a major city and their eventual political career.

Olivia knew with Daddy's money—*Don't be sexist. It could be Mommy's money.* I dug deeper into the file. Nope, I was right the first time. Daddy's money. With Daddy's money, Olivia didn't need a career. Her mother was demanding one hundred thousand dollars per month in combined child and spousal support, plus the house in Monteverde. She was willing to let Olivia's father keep the house in Aspen and the apartment in New York.

I was surprised this battle was still being fought in court. High end divorces usually settled privately. They must really hate each other. I dug deeper into the file. Olivia's mother accused Olivia's father of committing adultery with Olivia's former math tutor, who was now pregnant with his child. First child for the math tutor, third for Olivia's father. Olivia was her father's second child, and Olivia's mother was his second wife. The father's first wife lived in New York, and his son from his first marriage was a junior at Stanford. Olivia's father met Olivia's mother when she was working as the half-brother's nanny. I detected a pattern.

I was still deep into the allegations—Olivia's father accused Olivia's mother of having a same-sex relationship with her Pilates instructor thereby nullifying, at least in his mind, his adultery—when Janelle appeared in the doorway to my office.

I stuck a post-it onto the page I'd been reading and set the file down on my desk. "Rich people really are different from the rest of us."

She smirked. "You would know."

"You think *I'm* rich?" I waved my arm in front of me. "Look at this place." It was much nicer now than it had been the first time I'd seen it, but it still looked like a strip mall office. No one would confuse this space with a high-end law firm.

Janelle sat down on the chair across from my desk and sighed. "Whatever you say, Ms. I Don't Need the Money."

I slid my feet off the desk and sat up. "Yeah, because my husband died and left me millions of dollars."

"Sheesh, what he'd do for a living?"

"Accountant. And not the super expensive kind either. But he had a five million dollar life insurance policy."

"You bought a five million dollar life insurance policy?"

"Not me. Him. I didn't even know about it until after he died."

"Hold up," she said with her hands in the air. "Your husband bought a five million dollar life insurance policy and he didn't tell you?"

She was almost as incredulous as I'd been when I discovered it the week after his death. I'd went to the bank to retrieve the one million dollar policy that I knew about from our safe deposit box, and tucked behind it was a five million dollar policy I'd never seen before. "Nope."

"Damn," Janelle said.

We didn't know each other well enough for her to ask me what I knew she wanted to ask—why the hell would he do that? And I didn't offer an explanation because I had none.

I remembered trying to talk to my mother about it at the time, but she'd shut me down. "Jonah loved you and Amelia. This was just his way of taking care of you."

"But why didn't he *tell* me, Mom? Why keep it a secret?"

"Maybe because he didn't want to argue with you?"

We probably would've argued. The monthly premiums were high. I would've told him it was a waste of money. "We were partners, Mom. We would've discussed it. That's what partners do."

"Like you're *discussing* it with me now?"

I don't know why that accusation brought tears to my eyes, but it did. Although in those first few weeks after Jonah's and Amelia's deaths, I'd cried constantly with no provocation. And as soon as I'd started crying, my mom had hugged me and said, "Jonah bought it because he loved you. He provided for you. Don't go looking for trouble where none exists."

I'd wanted to believe her, so I did. It was easy to put it out of my mind because I'd taken the proceeds and deposited them into a savings account where the money was still sitting untouched. But now I couldn't avoid thinking about it again.

Was my mother right? Was I looking for trouble where none

existed? Or was trouble lurking all along and I just refused to see it? I'd told Jake earlier that Jonah and I hadn't kept secrets from each other, but that wasn't true. I hadn't kept secrets from Jonah, but he'd kept secrets from me. The question was why.

Chapter 35

I CAME HOME from the office early because Aunt Maddy was attending her first night of foster parent training. According to Janelle, it was a formality. All Aunt Maddy had to do was show up once a week and watch a couple of hours of bad videos from the eighties about kids in foster care. She could sleep through it or play on her phone the whole time because they didn't give the participants a test at the end. That didn't inspire confidence.

We fed the kids an early dinner and left them downstairs watching television while we went upstairs to my aunt's bedroom so she could get ready to leave.

"I stopped at the house after my appointment with Dr. Rubenstein today," I called out to my aunt, who was rummaging through her walk-in closet.

She emerged wearing gray slacks and a plain white bra, holding up two long-sleeve shirts on hangers—one solid and one striped. "Which one?" she asked.

"I like the stripes."

She stared at the striped shirt, tossed it onto the bed, and pulled the solid black shirt over her head. "It's better to be conservative. You never know."

"I don't really think it matters what you wear since you'll be sitting in a dark room watching videos all night. You could show up in your pajamas and they'd let you in."

She shrugged and returned to the closet.

"So the weirdest thing happened when I got to my house—Jake was there."

No response.

"Don't you think that's weird?" I called out.

Aunt Maddy reemerged from the closet, this time wearing a loafer on one foot and a low-heeled pump on the other. "Why is that weird? I thought you two still saw each other sometimes."

Aunt Maddy hadn't asked me about Jake since that night when I'd first brought MJ and Sofia home, and I hadn't volunteered any information. "Occasionally," I said. "But he always calls first. Today he just let himself into my house."

Aunt Maddy stopped staring at her mismatched shoes in the mirror and turned around. "He let himself into your house?"

Finally, the reaction I'd been waiting for. "Apparently, he has a key. And no, I didn't give it to him," I added before she could ask. "He says Jonah gave him a key to the house when we moved in. For emergencies."

"Oh, well, that makes sense," she said and returned to her closet. When she emerged twenty second later, she'd ditched the loafer and was now wearing two low-heeled pumps.

"In what way does that make sense?"

"You gave me a key for emergencies and Jonah gave one to his brother."

"I gave you a key because you live here. And Jonah knew. We'd talked about and he agreed you should have one."

Aunt Maddy looked at me in the mirror as she attached small silver hoops to her ears. "And you never discussed giving one to Jake?"

"Nope."

Aunt Maddy stopped staring in the mirror and turned around to face me. "And you're angry at Jonah because he didn't tell you?"

"I'm not angry," I said, even though I definitely sounded angry, even to my own ears. "I just don't understand. I mean, why wouldn't he have told me? Why keep it a secret?"

She chuckled. "Sweetie, he probably did tell you and you forgot."

"No, I think I would remember."

"Your Uncle Ben used to forget things all the time, then swear I never told him. I'd threatened to start recording all our conversations if he didn't start writing things down."

"This is different."

"No, Sweetie, it's not. You're mad at Jonah for dying, but since it's silly to be mad at someone for dying, you've decided you're mad at him because he didn't tell you he gave his brother a key."

"I'm not mad!" I shouted. "I just don't understand why he was hiding things from me."

Aunt Maddy sat down next to me on the bed and reached for my hand. "Obviously, you're upset about this. Do you need me to cancel and stay home tonight?"

"No," I pouted.

"I could take the class later. I think the social worker said there's another session starting in two weeks."

"No, go to the class. I'm fine."

"If you're sure," she said, standing up.

"I'm sure."

She grabbed her purse off the dresser and slipped it over her shoulder. "In that case, I usually start Sofia's bath at seven. She likes to blow bubbles together or play with her bath toys but don't let her stay in the water too long because I like to read to her for half an hour before bed. She'll want you to read *Caps For*

Sale first because that's her favorite, but save *Goodnight Moon* for last because that's the one that puts her to sleep."

I smiled thinking back to the first time I left Amelia alone with Jonah when I made my first post-partum trip to the grocery store. Then I remembered I'd never see either one of them again and my smile disappeared.

I tried hard not to think about Amelia as I bathed Sofia, dressed her in her new *Peppa Pig* pajamas, then laid next to her in her bed and read her book after book until she finally fell asleep—but I failed. Sofia must've sensed my mood because at one point she reached over and hugged me and told me not to be so sad.

It was a relief when Sofia finally fell asleep, and I could go back downstairs. I found MJ sitting at the dining room table with a math book propped open in front of him and a pencil in his hand.

"More homework?" I asked, surprised. I thought he'd finished his homework at the office this afternoon. That was our routine now. He'd walk to my office after school each day, and I'd send him out to buy us lunch (even though he'd previously eaten lunch at school). After he finished eating, Janelle or I would give him work to do, usually photocopying or filing. When he finished, he'd sit at the desk in the reception area and do his homework or play on his phone until it was time to leave.

MJ blushed, which was not the reaction I was expecting, so I leaned over his shoulder for a closer look. I thought maybe I'd find a *Playboy* or *Sport's Illustrated* swimsuit edition hidden inside the textbook, but it was just trigonometry. "I thought you were taking algebra."

"I am," he said. "This is extra."

"Extra credit?"

"No, just extra."

"So you're taking two math classes?"

"No."

I sighed. I was too tired to play the twenty questions game. I pulled out the chair next to him and sat down. "MJ, if you're not taking trigonometry, why are you working on math problems from a trigonometry text book?"

He shrugged. "I dunno."

"You don't know?" I said, losing what little patience I had left. I understood why every parent hated the teenage years. "I think you do know."

"I just like math, okay. It's fun."

Math is fun? "So you're some kind of math genius and you're just now telling me?"

He rolled his eyes. "I like math. Don't make such a big deal over it."

"Who's your math teacher?"

He crossed his arms over his chest and stared at his textbook. "You don't know him."

"I know I don't know him. That's why I'm asking for his name. Because if you're gifted in math, I think I need to get to know him."

MJ snorted. "I ain't gifted."

"It's *not* gifted, not ain't gifted. And how do you know you're not? Have you ever been tested?"

He shook his head and picked up his pencil again, and I made a mental note to contact MJ's school the next day.

Chapter 36

Principal Ramirez stared at me from the other side of her huge wooden desk that looked like it had been at the school since it opened, which according to the plaque on the wall outside the entrance was in 1948. "So who are you to MJ?"

"An interested party," I replied.

"I don't know what that means," Ms. Ramirez said.

She was younger than I thought she'd be. I remembered school principals being old, but maybe that was because when you're a child, all adults seem old. I guessed she was around my age and very pretty. I wondered if that was an asset or a liability when dealing with teenage boys.

I smiled. "It's complicated."

Ms. Ramirez didn't smile back. "I'm sure it is. Many of our students have complicated home lives. Are you MJ's guardian?"

"Not officially. I don't know if you're aware of the situation, but MJ's mother is...not able to take care of him and his sister right now, so they're in foster care with me and my aunt." Now that Janelle had contacted CPS, there was no need to keep it a secret.

"So you're his foster parent?"

"Technically, that would be my aunt. But I'm helping out because I live there too." I thought that would raise an eyebrow —why would a grown woman be living with her aunt?—but it didn't.

"Then I can't help you. Without a parent's or guardian's permission, I'm not allowed to share a student's information."

"So you can't tell me if he's ever been tested for a gifted program?"

Principal Ramirez smiled, but it was to cover for her laugh.

"Why is that funny?"

"I'm sorry," Ms. Ramirez said. "It's not the question I was expecting. Or, at least, not one I usually get."

I knew what she was thinking—I was a "Karen" coming in here demanding that MJ be tested for a gifted program, which probably didn't even exist in this school, when she had students dealing with homelessness and food insecurity. But I didn't care. "I'm trying to help MJ. He's a good kid; a smart kid. Very smart, in fact. I caught him doing trigonometry last night *for fun.* If he's really good at math, I don't think we should ignore that."

"We're not ignoring it," she said, instantly defensive. She glanced down at MJ's file. "He has Mr. Guardia for math. He's one of our best teachers."

"Is that an AP math class?"

Her jaw clenched and I had no doubt she'd be sharing this conversation with her colleagues after I left. *You would not believe this woman,* she'd tell them, and they'd all laugh. But to me she said, "We don't offer AP classes at this school, but I can assure you, we try our best for all our students. Is that all, Ms. Hughes?"

Clearly, I was being dismissed. "Is it possible to get Mr. Guardia's phone number?" Maybe he'd be more open to helping MJ.

She scribbled something on a notepad, ripped off the sheet of paper, and handed it to me.

I glanced down at a school email address.

"We don't give out teacher phone numbers. Emails are available on the website." She stood up and escorted me to her office door.

TODAY WHEN MJ delivered our lunch, instead of eating at my own desk, I joined him in the reception area. I sat on the mint green sofa with my cup of Greek yogurt, while he sat at the reception desk and inhaled a meatball sub.

"I met your principal today," I said, scraping the bottom of the cup with my plastic spoon.

He swallowed hard before responding. "Ms. Ramirez? She's fine."

"She told me they don't offer AP classes at your school."

"What's an AP class?"

"Advanced Placement. It helps you get into college."

He took another huge bite of his sub.

"I was thinking, have you ever thought about going to a different high school?" I'd emailed Mr. Guardia when I returned to the office, but I hadn't heard back yet and I didn't know if I ever would. Rather than do nothing, I spent some time this morning researching local high schools.

"The teachers at my old school said we all go to Morris High."

Technically, that was correct. Theodore J. Morris High School was the only high school in this school district. But there were better school districts in the area and private schools too. The high school in The Hills was top rated, but getting MJ in there would be tricky since I wasn't actually MJ's legal guardian. Enrolling him in a private school would be easier if I was willing to pay for it, which I was. I decided it would be a good use of the money from Jonah's life insurance policy.

"I meant a private school."

MJ dropped what was left of his sub onto the wax paper wrapper. "You know I ain't got no money."

"They give scholarships. Or some of them do." I thought he might be more receptive to the idea of a scholarship than my offer to pay.

"To people like me?"

"Yes, MJ, that's who the scholarships are for. People who can't afford to pay."

"I mean they give 'em to Black people?"

"Yes." If anything, being a person of color would boost his chances. All the private schools liked to tout their diversity stats.

He seemed to consider the idea. "Would I be the only Black person?"

I'd never toured the local private schools, not even the preschools, although I had intended to when Amelia turned two. But I had toured the local daycare centers. Extrapolating I said, "Probably not the only one, but the school will likely be mostly white."

"Nah," he said. "I don't want to leave my friends."

It could be about his friends. Or it could be that he didn't want to be one of a handful of Black kids in an overwhelmingly white school. For the first time since that mad dash to the pediatrician's office when everyone told me I was in over my head I felt like maybe they were right. I was a white woman whose only experience raising a child was with an infant. What did I know about raising a Black teenage boy?

But I wanted MJ to have a good education. That was one of the primary reasons Jonah and I had moved to Santa Veneta, so our future children could attend good schools. I wished the options weren't either leave him at a low-rated school where he felt comfortable or send him to a highly-rated school where he might feel out of place. But even without touring every local school, I knew enough about Santa Veneta to know there were no schools, public or private, with a truly diverse student body. All the high-performing schools in the area were majority white and Asian, and all the low-performing schools were majority Black and Latino. In that respect, Santa Veneta was no different from San Francisco or LA.

I stood up and tossed my empty yogurt cup into the trash. I'd ask Janelle. Maybe she'd have some insights.

Chapter 37

I received an email from Mr. Guardia that evening. He offered to meet with me before school the next morning. MJ wasn't happy about it, as much because he had to get out of bed half an hour early as my meeting with his teacher "for no reason." But I didn't give him a choice.

When I entered Mr. Guardia's classroom, he stood up and shook my hand. Instead of returning to his seat behind his teacher's desk, he sat down at a student desk and motioned for me to slide into one too. He wore jeans and a button-down shirt with a tie, and his olive skin was smooth and unlined.

"Your MJ's foster mother?" he asked.

I'd been purposely vague in my email because I didn't want him to shut me down like the school principal had. "It's an emergency placement. We're in the process of getting certified."

"And you're concerned about MJ's math grade? Because I can assure you that you have nothing to worry about. MJ's an A student, at least in math."

"I know he's good in math. My concern is the opposite, that maybe the school isn't maximizing MJ's potential."

Karen-alert. I could see it in the almost-smile that played on

Mr. Guardia's lips. But when he responded his tone was friendly. "I try my best, Ms. Hughes."

"I'm sure you do, Mr. Guardia. I didn't mean it as a criticism of you."

"Just a criticism of the school?"

I was about to launch into a defense of my position when Mr. Guardia gave me a genuine smile. "It's okay. I know what you meant. This school doesn't exactly have a reputation for maximizing students' potential. If that's what you're looking for, you need to move up to The Hills. I hear they have an excellent high school."

I laughed. "I actually own a house in The Hills."

"That does not surprise me. No offense intended," he added after registering the expression on my face.

I laughed again. "Okay, now that we've both insulted each other, can we work together to help MJ?"

"Of course. And I apologize if I insulted you. That really was not my intent."

"And it really wasn't my intent to insult you either. But let's be honest about the fact that this is not a great school. The test scores are well below the State average, which aren't exactly high to begin with. I don't think anyone, except maybe Ms. Ramirez, would claim the students at this school are getting a good education."

"We try our best, Ms. Hughes, but we have limited resources. Unlike our counterparts in The Hills, we don't have gala fundraisers where our students' families donate thousands of dollars to make up for State budget cuts. And I doubt many of the kids in The Hills are dealing with the serious issues in their home lives that many of our students are. It's not a fair comparison."

"I know that, and I agree with you. It's not fair. Every kid deserves a good education, regardless of their zip code. But I'm one person, Mr. Guardia. I can't help every child. But I can help MJ."

Mr. Guardia nodded. "I've been trying to help MJ too. He is far ahead of the other students, so rather than have him sit there for fifty minutes staring out the window, I give him extra assignments. By the time this school year ends, he'll essentially be a year ahead in math."

"When I met with Ms. Ramirez, I asked her if MJ had ever been tested for a gifted program and she basically laughed at me."

Mr. Guardia didn't laugh but he did smile. "This district doesn't have a gifted program."

"And no AP classes either. So what do you do with the really smart kids?"

"We try to keep them engaged. And some of us look for alternatives."

"Alternative schools?"

He nodded. "That's not a popular idea around here. Some people think we should keep the best students here to try to raise everyone up, and by helping one student get into a better school, it means we're giving up on those that remain."

"Is that what you think?"

"I think in an ideal world, every kid would go to a great school. But in an ideal world, every kid would have a stable home life and enough food to eat, and that hasn't happened yet either. So until that happens, I help how I can."

"I want MJ to go to a better school but he doesn't want to leave."

"That doesn't surprise me," Mr. Guardia said. "Kids never want to leave their friends."

"I know, but if I could get him to consider it and he came to you for advice, would you advise him to go?"

"Yes, although I'd be sorry to see him leave. He's my best student."

WHEN I ARRIVED at the office Janelle was already sitting at her desk. "Got a minute?" I asked.

"Sure," she said, looking away from her computer screen. "Have you met with Olivia yet?"

"I have an appointment with her at her mom's house this afternoon."

"Great," she said and held out two more files. "Read 'em first. Then we'll talk."

I took the files and sat down in one of her guest chairs. "I need some advice."

"About Olivia?"

"No, about MJ." I told Janelle about my meeting with MJ's math teacher and the school principal the day before. She laughed when I told her I asked if he'd ever been tested for a gifted program. "You know what they're saying about you, don't you?"

"I can imagine, but all I care about is helping MJ. The school principal's useless, but his math teacher seems willing."

"That's great," Janelle said.

"It would be if MJ actually wanted to go to another school. But when I floated the idea, he shot me down. He says he doesn't want to leave his friends."

"Of course, he doesn't want to leave his friends. What teenager does?"

"Yeah, but I'm not sure that's the real reason, or, at least, not the only reason." Janelle leaned back in her chair and waited for me to continue. "He asked me if he'd be the only Black student."

Janelle paused before she spoke. "He's probably never been in a setting where he's the only Black person, except maybe at the mall, and then he had a security guard following him around the store checking he didn't steal anything."

"So you think I should stop pushing him to go to a better school?"

"Hell no!"

"But I don't want to force him to go."

Janelle snorted. "He's a teenager, Grace. Thinking about his future means his next meal. But *you* can't force him to do anything because *you* are not his legal guardian."

I knew that, of course, I just forgot sometimes. "So who do I talk to about this? His social worker?"

"No, social workers can't be educational rights holders. And neither can the child's attorney," she added before I could ask. "When we go to the next hearing, we can request the judge appoint your aunt since she's his temporary legal guardian."

"In MJ's case, maybe. For Sofia, she's basically her new mom."

Janelle looked at me quizzically. "Is that a problem?"

"No, I just meant..." What did I mean? Wasn't it good that my aunt had essentially taken over care of Sofia? What would I have done if she hadn't? "She takes the lead with Sofia and I take the lead with MJ."

"That's great," Janelle said. "Then the emergency placement is working out for both of you."

That was one way to look at it. Janelle was Sofia's lawyer, so if she wasn't concerned, I wouldn't be either. I stood up to leave, but when I headed to the door Janelle said, "A piece of advice. If MJ's really going to be a lawyer someday, he needs to start getting used to being the only Black person in the room."

Chapter 38

I WOUND my way through Monteverde Estates and stopped at the bottom of a long gated driveway. A few minutes later I was standing in the foyer of Oliva Baylor's mother's seven thousand square foot house. I'd looked it up on Zillow before I left the office so I already knew it had six bedrooms, eight bathrooms, a sprawling front lawn, a pool, a tennis court, and a spectacular mountain view. But from the foyer, all I could see was the formal living room and a kitchen down the hall.

The housekeeper had let me in, but as soon as she'd closed the door behind me, a barefoot woman wearing black yoga pants and a matching sports bra appeared. "Claire Baylor," she said, extending her hand. "Olivia's mother."

Her eyes were green, her hair golden, and nothing on her jiggled except for her breasts, which may or may not have been real. From a distance I would've guessed she was in her mid-twenties. But when we shook hands, I could see the fine lines around her eyes and realized she had to be nearing forty.

"Can I get you something to drink?" she asked. "Water, coffee, juice? Or Anna can make you a smoothie, if you'd like."

"Water would be great, thanks." It was hotter up in the hills of Monteverde than it had been down in the flats of Santa Veneta where my office was located.

Claire spun on her toes and headed down the hallway towards the kitchen so I followed. She pulled open both doors of the extra-wide Subzero refrigerator and stared inside. "Flat, sparkling, fruit infused, or coconut water?"

"Flat," I replied.

She turned to me. "Are you sure? Coconut water is great for hydration. My facialist swears by it."

Did my skin look like it needed hydration? Probably. I still hadn't gotten back into my skincare regime from Before. Half the time I left the house without even applying sunscreen first, a cardinal sin in sunny Southern California. "Flat's fine, thanks."

She shrugged and handed me a bottle of spring water, then opened a coconut water for herself and took a sip. "Have a seat," she said, motioning to the barstools lined up at the marble-countered kitchen island.

I slid onto the closest stool, but she remained standing on the other side.

"So what happened to the other lawyer?" she asked. "What was her name again? Janice?"

"Janelle," I replied. "We work together. She's really busy right now, so she's transferring some of her cases to me."

"Lucky us." She smiled.

I smiled back. "Is Olivia home?"

"She's upstairs. But I thought we could talk first."

I remembered what Janelle had told me about the parents always trying to get you on their side. "I would love to, but I'm really pressed for time today. I'd be happy to call your lawyer and set up a meeting for the three of us for next week, if you'd like."

We both knew that meeting would never happen. It was the legal equivalent of let's do lunch. If she couldn't pressure me without her lawyer present, there was no point in talking to me at all. "I'll go get Olivia."

A few minutes later a sullen teenager shuffled into the kitchen. She had a coltish figure, long pink hair, and her mother's green eyes.

"Hey," she said.

I slid off my barstool and offered her my hand. "I'm Grace Hughes, your new lawyer."

She stared at my outstretched hand, keeping her own hands tucked into the pockets of her jeans shorts, until I finally dropped mine. "What happened to my old lawyer?"

"She's busy with other cases so I'm taking over this one. Is there somewhere private where we can talk?"

"You can sit outside, if you'd like," Olivia's mother replied. "There's shade by the pool."

"Is that where you'd like to go?" I asked Olivia.

She shrugged and headed toward the wall of sliding glass doors. I picked up my briefcase and followed. Olivia led us past the pool and tennis court to a table and chairs under a bougainvillea covered pergola. We both sat down, me with my legs crossed and her with her knees pulled into her chest and her arms wrapped tightly around them.

I pulled a pad and pen from my briefcase and set them on my lap. "Tell me about yourself."

She rolled her eyes dramatically. "Don't you people talk to each other? I already told the last lawyer all this."

"Yes, we talk. And yes, I read your file. But I'd like to hear it from you."

"Why?"

"Because I'm your lawyer, Olivia. So I'd like to hear from *you* about this situation and how—"

"It sucks, okay? I can't wait until I turn eighteen and then I can do what I want."

"You're fifteen now, right?"

"Shouldn't you know that already?"

I tried to keep the annoyance out of my voice. "Yes, just confirming."

"I can *confirm* that I'm fifteen years old. Happy?"

I placed my pad and pen on the table and took a deep breath. When I thought about being an advocate for children, this was not what I'd envisioned. My pro bono clients in LA had been underprivileged kids. They were wary at first, but once they realized that I genuinely wanted to help them they were appreciative. This was my first time representing an entitled teenager, and now I understood why Janelle was only too happy to pass these cases off to me. "If you want my help, drop the attitude."

"If you really want to help me, get my parents to let me live on my own."

I couldn't suppress my laugh. "Olivia, you're fifteen. That's not going to happen."

"Then I guess you can't 'help me,'" she replied with the air quotes. She unfolded her legs and placed her bare feet on the ground. "Are we done?"

"No. And if you don't drop the attitude, I'm going to recommend to the judge that your parents send you to military school."

"You can't do that!"

"Oh yes, I can. I can make whatever recommendations I think are in your best interest. And right now, I think that means learning some respect. So how about cooperating?"

She rolled her eyes but pulled her feet back up onto her chair. "Fine. What do you want to know?"

"Let's start with who you'd prefer to live with—your mother or your father?"

"Neither!"

"Why?"

"Well, you've met my mother."

"Yes, and?"

"Duh," she said.

I gritted my teeth and took another deep breath. "Maybe you could explain to me why living with your mother's so awful. Does she drink or use drugs?"

"No, she says alcohol's too fattening. I don't know about the drugs. If she's using, it's not around me."

"I think if your mother was a drug addict you'd know."

Olivia shrugged.

"Any abuse—and I don't mean enforcing a curfew or cutting off your credit card."

Olivia let out a laugh. "Well, when you put it that way."

I reminded myself what it was like to be a teenager. You weren't a child anymore but you weren't an adult either, and no one understood the pressure you felt. And when I was a teenager, everyone didn't all have cell phones and 24/7 social media. I placed my pen and pad back on the table and pulled my knees up to my chest too. "I get it. Mothers are annoying. Mine is too and I'm a lot older than you. But is your mom annoying like all moms are annoying, forcing you to do stuff you don't want to do? Or is it more than that?"

Instead of another sarcastic retort, Olivia seemed to ponder the question. "It's like she just doesn't care, you know?"

"Doesn't care about your feelings? Or what you do? Or your likes and dislikes?"

"All of it. You know the only reason she's even fighting for custody is to stick it to my dad. I honestly think if he gave her enough money, she'd agree to never see me again."

In that moment she reminded me of MJ. Obviously, her circumstances were much better than his but, at bottom, she was a child who felt unloved. "I'm really sorry to hear that, Olivia. I know we just met, and you obviously know your relationship with your mother much better than I do, but do you want to know what I think?"

"What?" she asked in a tone that was much less sarcastic than I'd expected.

"I think you talk tough, but on the inside, you're a really sweet kid."

"Seriously?"

"Yes. Am I wrong? Are you really a raving bitch on the inside too?"

"O-M-G! I can't believe you just said that to me."

I laughed. "Why? You think lawyers don't curse?" Or was it that no one had ever called her out on her bullshit before?

"Not at me. In front of me, they're all, like, stick up their butt. Especially that Janelle lady."

I didn't think of Janelle as being uptight, but I imagined she might appear that way with clients, especially a client like Olivia. I normally had a more professional demeanor with clients too. This was a first for me as well. "I promise when we go to court, I'll act all proper in front of the judge. But when it's just the two of us, I think we can relax. Unless you'd rather I—"

"Act like a priss? No thanks. I like you better this way. And you better not tell the judge to send me to military school."

"Then you better answer my questions."

"Fine," she said and uncrossed her arms. "But I still get to call you out if you ask me something stupid."

"Deal."

Over the course of an hour I learned that Olivia's mother spent more time out of the house—shopping, Pilates, dinner with friends—than she spent at home. Olivia's mother didn't have a job, but she still managed to fill her days and nights with Olivia-free activities. When Olivia was at her father's house, a nearby property he'd moved to after he split with Olivia's mother, she didn't see him much either, especially not after Olivia's math tutor had moved in.

"Do you like her?"

She shrugged. "She's okay. I liked her better when she was my tutor."

Not surprising. She probably blamed the tutor for her parents' divorce. "Do you have a new tutor?" I'd checked her transcripts, and she'd gotten a "D" in math last quarter so, apparently, she still needed one.

"No. My mom said I can only have old lady tutors from now on, and they're soooo boring."

"What about a male tutor?"

She shook her head. "My mother doesn't trust me around men."

"Maybe it's the men she doesn't trust." Especially if she wore as little clothes with them as she wore with me. Her cut-off jean shorts and halter top didn't leave much to the imagination.

Oliva shrugged.

"Is there someone at your school who could tutor you? Another student, maybe?" I remembered my high school had a peer-to-peer tutoring program where kids could sign up to tutor other kids. Usually it was the geeky boys who would volunteer so they could get the cool girls to talk to them but, occasionally, it was a geeky girl tutoring one of the jock boys. The pairings always seemed to be opposite sex.

Olivia looked at me like I'd just suggested she sprout wings and fly. "We don't, like, tutor each other. We just hire people."

Of course, they did. "Have you ever considered hiring a tutor closer to your own age? Maybe then they wouldn't be so boring."

"I told you, my mom said I can only have old lady tutors."

"Because she doesn't trust men. But what if it was a boy your own age? Do you think she'd be okay with that?"

She shrugged. "Maybe. You know someone cool?"

Of course, I was thinking of MJ. I didn't know if he was cool by Oliva's standards, but he definitely had swagger. And I thought he could help Olivia and not just in math. It would be good for her to spend time with someone who didn't have everything handed to them on a silver platter. It would be good for MJ too. If nothing else, it would provide him with a real job. Most days Janelle and I had a hard time finding anything for him to do.

"Maybe," I replied. "I'd need to talk to him about it first."

"Is he hot?" she asked and broke into a fit of giggles, acting for the first time like a fifteen-year-old girl instead of one several years older.

"On second thought, let me run this by your mother first."

OLIVIA'S MOTHER said yes immediately. I didn't know if it was because she genuinely wanted to help her daughter in math or if she thought if she acquiesced to my request that would mean I'd be on her side. Her only requirement was that they be supervised. She didn't want Olivia spending time alone with a male of any age.

"Do you want him to come to the house?" I asked. I didn't know how MJ would get here. There were no bus stops in this part of town, and it would be too expensive to Uber, but maybe Olivia's parents would be willing to pay for his travel too.

"No," Claire said as if that was the dumbest question she'd ever heard. "I don't have time to supervise."

I didn't point out that since she didn't have a job, she could probably find a way to fit it into her busy Pilates/shopping schedule, if she actually wanted to. "Can your housekeeper supervise? She's here anyway."

Claire let out a laugh as if it that suggestion was almost as ridiculous as my previous one. "No, Anna has her own work to do. This really feels like a school thing to me. Why don't you call them and have them work it out. They found the last two tutors."

"You want *me* to call the school?" That seemed like a parent task.

"My husband's paying you, isn't he?"

"Yes, to represent your daughter's legal interests not to arrange her schedule."

Claire sighed dramatically. "Honestly, Grace, are you going to be this difficult about everything? You're almost as bad as Janice."

I didn't bother correcting her.

"Just call the school and have them figure out. And make sure my husband gets the bill." Then she grabbed another coconut water from the refrigerator and flounced out of the room.

Chapter 39

I WAITED until that evening to run my idea by MJ. I sat down next to him on the couch, and once the show he'd been watching ended, I shut off the TV. "I found a new job for you."

"Why do I need a new job?" he asked. "You firing me?"

"Of course not. This would only be one or two days a week. You can still work for me and Janelle the other days." Although "work" was a relative term. He mostly did his homework and played games on his phone.

"What's the job?"

"Math tutor."

MJ laughed. "I can't be no math tutor."

"Why not? You're good at math."

"Don't you have to be a teacher or something?"

"You don't have to be a teacher to help someone with their homework. And the pay is good." That got his attention.

"How much?"

"Double your hourly rate working for me." It was still a third of what Olivia's parents had paid her previous tutor.

"For real?"

"Yes. But you have to help her with her homework. You can't just sit around chatting her up for an hour."

"It's a girl?"

"Yes. Is that a problem?"

"Not for me."

"Good. Now I just have to figure out where you guys are going to meet."

"How about here?"

I glanced around my aunt's living room, which was now filled with dolls and Legos and toys with flashing lights that played tunes that stuck in your head. "Someplace less distracting I think."

A library would be ideal, but one where they didn't shush you for talking. I wondered if Olivia's school had such a library, or maybe an empty classroom where one of the teachers could supervise. I was sure I could get Olivia's parents to pay the teacher too.

"I'll figure it out."

MJ nodded and picked up the remote again, but he didn't turn on the TV.

"Is there anything you wanted to talk about?" I asked. I could think of so many topics—school, his mom, his living situation—but I'd found that I could usually get more information out of MJ if I let him come to me.

"You know this girl?" he asked. "The one I'm gonna tutor."

"I just met her today. I'm representing her in her parents' divorce."

"So she got her own lawyer, just like me and Sofia?"

That's not how it usually worked in divorce cases, but in this case, "Yes. Why?"

He shrugged. "Just wondering what she's like."

"Is that guy code for is she pretty?" We both laughed, but

MJ didn't deny it. "Smart, like you, but not in math. Nice when she wants to be. And cute."

"Cute?"

"Think Taylor Swift but with pink hair." I waited for him to say more, but he didn't, so I finally asked, "Is there anything else? You can tell me anything, you know."

"Nope," he said and turned on the TV.

I CALLED Olivia's school the next morning and was told that the school maintained a list of recommended tutors, which they would be happy to send me, but that they didn't arrange for sessions or provide office space or supervision. "That's the responsibility of the student's parent," the head of school's assistant politely told me. "Or their staff."

I laughed to myself as I hung up. Apparently, I was now "staff." Not the role I'd envisioned for myself when I'd taken this job. I thought I'd actually be helping kids in need. But on the positive side, this job had forced me back out into the world again. And I no longer spent all my time ruminating over Jonah and Amelia. That was a plus.

WHEN DR. RUBENSTEIN escorted me into her office that afternoon I switched my phone to vibrate and took my usual spot on the couch.

"How are you feeling today?" she asked.

"Fine," I said automatically. "How are you?"

"Good," she said. "But I'm not the one who attempted suicide a few months ago."

I laughed. If Dr. Stetler had been more like Dr. Rubenstein, I might not have hated the Wellstone Center so much.

"Did you go to your house like you promised?"

"I did, actually."

She seemed surprised. "And?"

"And Jake was there."

"Your brother-in-law?"

"Yes."

I expected her to ask me why he was there or, at least, how I felt seeing him there, but she didn't. She just sat and waited and, eventually, I told her everything.

"You seem quite upset about this," she said.

"Of course, I'm upset about it." I'd put it out of my mind for a few days, but now that I was forced to think about it again, I was triggered anew. "I *still* don't know why he was there."

"And that bothers you?"

"Yes. It also bothers me that Jonah gave him a key and didn't tell me. Don't you think that's weird?"

She shrugged. "Your aunt could be right. It's possible you forgot. Or maybe Jonah purposely didn't tell you because he didn't want to argue about it."

"Now you sound like my mother!"

"You talked to your mother about this too?"

"No, but that's what she said when I told her about the life insurance policy."

"What life insurance policy?"

I realized I'd never told Dr. Rubenstein about the second life insurance policy. It's not that I'd purposely kept it from her; she and I never talked about money. All she ever wanted to discuss was my feelings. So today I told her about the five million dollar life insurance policy too.

"That is odd," she said.

"Thank you! My mom and my aunt both think I'm just looking for trouble. That Jonah bought it because he loved me and Amelia and it was his way of taking care of us."

"Is that what you think?"

"I think I didn't know my husband as well as I thought I did."

I CHECKED my phone as I was leaving Dr. Rubenstein's office. I had two voicemails—one from Aunt Maddy and another from Janelle—and a text from MJ. All three asked me to contact them right away. I texted MJ first and when he didn't respond I called Aunt Maddy, who didn't pick up. It was Janelle who answered her phone. "It's MJ. He's been in a fight."

Chapter 40

As soon I heard the words "MJ" and "fight," my heart started pounding. "What happened? Is he okay?"

"He's still at the school," Janelle replied. "So I assume so."

"You *assume so*?"

"If he was seriously injured, he'd be at the hospital. We have a meeting with him and the school principal in fifteen minutes."

"Who's we?" I asked.

"Your aunt. She's MJ's legal guardian so that's who the school called. Madeline called me. She said she tried you but you didn't pick up."

"I was in a meeting."

"We both thought you'd want to be there," she continued.

"I do," I said, racing through the parking lot to my car. "Do we know how it started? I mean, MJ's such a good kid. Is he being bullied?"

"I don't think so based on the school's reaction."

"What do you mean their reaction?"

"The principal's threatening disciplinary action."

"Disciplinary action? Against MJ? Why?"

I heard a beeping sound and knew it was Janelle's call waiting. "I've got to take this. I'll see you at the school."

I SPED to MJ's high school and found him sitting on a bench outside the principal's office, wedged between Janelle on one side and my aunt and Sofia on the other. The collar of his shirt was torn, one side of his face was swollen, and he had cotton stuffed up both nostrils.

"Oh my god," I said, rushing to MJ. "Are you okay?"

"Stay calm," Janelle said, as he nodded.

"Stay calm? Look at him." I turned to MJ. "Who did this to you?"

But before either of them could answer the door to the inner office opened and Principal Ramirez stepped out. "You can come in now."

The five of us filed into the principal's office, Janelle leading, me in the rear, and Aunt Maddy, Sofia, and MJ sandwiched between us. I was surprised to see Mr. Guardia there, perched on the edge of a low bookshelf, leaving the three plastic chairs facing Ms. Ramirez's desk empty.

"Do you have any more chairs?" I asked.

"I don't think we can fit any more," Mr. Guardia replied.

He was right. The office was small and it was already a tight squeeze with just the three.

"I'll wait outside with Sofia," Aunty Maddy said.

"Madeline, you're his legal guardian," Janelle said. "You should be here."

Aunt Maddy turned to me and I could tell by her expression that she would rather be anywhere else. I said, "I can take your place if you want, if it's okay with MJ."

"I want Grace to stay," MJ replied.

Janelle shrugged her assent, so I stayed and Aunt Maddy and Sofia retreated.

Janelle and I sat on either end with MJ between us. Principal Ramirez returned to her chair and clasped her hands together on her desk before she spoke. "As I told MJ's foster mother on the phone, MJ attacked another student today."

"He punched me first," MJ cried.

Principal Ramirez ignored MJ's outburst and continued addressing Janelle. "The other boy's mother just called from the hospital. MJ dislocated his shoulder."

"Yeah, after he hit me," MJ yelled, then turned to me. "He hit me first, I swear."

"I believe you," I said and swiveled back to Principal Ramirez. "You have security cameras, don't you?" I noticed two small monitors in the corner of her office showing different access points to the school. "Let's look at the recording."

"We have a few security cameras," she acknowledged, "but they don't cover every inch of the school grounds and this incident was not caught on tape."

"How convenient."

She ignored my remark and continued. "This is not MJ's first altercation with this boy, and his parents are considering filing a police report."

"Then you need to preserve all your security camera footage," Janelle said. "Both from today and from the day of the last altercation."

"I don't know if we still have footage from that day," Principal Ramirez said. "That fight happened earlier in the year."

"And who started the last fight?" I asked.

"We don't know," Principal Ramirez said. "That one wasn't on camera either."

"But I witnessed it," Mr. Guardia said. "And I don't think MJ was the aggressor."

Principal Ramirez glared at Mr. Guardia before turning her attention back to me and Janelle. "Our investigation was inconclusive. We suspended both boys for two days and recommended counseling."

"Did they receive counseling?" Janelle asked.

"Yes, they each met with the school counselor," Principal Ramirez replied.

"How often?" Janelle asked.

"I believe it was once each," Principal Ramirez said.

"Once?" I said. "You thought one session with the school counselor was going to fix this?" I'd met with Dr. Rubenstein more than a dozen times and I was nowhere near ready to stop.

"There are over a thousand students in this school, Ms. Hughes. We don't have the resources to offer long-term counseling to each one. We rely on the parents for that, if it's needed."

"Even though you know MJ's mother's missing and his father's dead?"

Principal Ramirez turned back to Janelle. "We'll be suspending MJ for five days. If there's a third incident, he'll be looking at possible expulsion."

"Expulsion!" I cried. "You would expel a student for defending himself?"

"I can assure you, Ms. Hughes, I'm following all of the district's policies and procedures."

"Maybe the district needs to reevaluate its policies and procedures."

Principal Ramirez's nostrils flared, but she didn't reply. Instead, she turned back to Janelle. "Do you have any other questions?"

"Not at this time," Janelle said. "But I'll be sending you a formal request to preserve all security camera footage."

Principal Ramirez nodded and stood up. Janelle, MJ, and I filed out of her office in silence.

"How did it go?" Aunt Maddy asked, looking up from the bench where she and Sofia had been waiting.

"Let's talk outside," Janelle said and motioned for us to follow her.

Janelle filled in Aunt Maddy as we all walked to Aunt Maddy's car, but MJ and I hung back so we could talk separately.

"How's the nose?" I asked.

"Okay," he replied.

"Maybe we should go the ER and have it x-rayed."

"Nah, I'm good."

I stopped walking and MJ did too. "Let me see it," I said and gently placed my hands on either side of his head. "I don't think it's broken." Although all I could really say for sure was that it wasn't bent.

"It's not," he replied and pulled the blood-stained cotton out of each nostril before sniffing loudly. "See, I can breathe."

"I'm not sure that proves anything. I'll call the pediatrician's office and see if she can squeeze us in." I pulled my phone out of my purse and started walking again.

MJ tapped my shoulder, and I stopped and turned around. "Thanks," he said.

"For what?" I replied. "You still got suspended."

"Thanks for sticking up for me."

"Of course, I'm going to stick up for you, MJ. That's what parents do. I know I'm not your parent, but I'm sure if your mother was here, she would've done the same."

"The last time they called my mom, and she never showed up."

I reached out and squeezed MJ's hand. "I'm sorry, MJ. You deserve better than what you've gotten."

After a few seconds I let go of his hand and started walking again.

"Hey, Grace," MJ said.

I stopped and turned around.

"Can I, um, give you a hug?"

I didn't wait for him to approach me. I threw my arms around MJ and buried my face in his shoulder. I didn't want him to see me cry.

Please, please, please, let his mother never come back.

Chapter 41

THE PEDIATRICIAN CONFIRMED that MJ's nose wasn't broken and the bruise on his cheek would heal on its own, but that only relieved my anxiety over his physical condition. I was still worried about his mental state. When I asked Janelle if Child Protective Services would arrange for individual counseling sessions for MJ, she actually laughed. I'd have to find him a therapist on my own. I wondered if I should get one for Sofia too, although she was still so young and seemed to be doing okay with my aunt.

I was also concerned how I was going to keep MJ busy for a week without school. But that proved not to be a problem. Janelle's computer crashed the next morning, and he spent the day helping Janelle recover her files. Then he researched specs for her and went with her to the store to buy a new one. After Janelle's new computer was up and running, MJ cleaned out the gutters at Aunt Maddy's house, and even worked a few odd jobs for Mike Murphy.

"You're such a good kid," I said to him while we were eating lunch together in the office on his last day of suspension. "I still can't believe you were suspended for fighting, not once but twice. How did this happen?"

I meant it as a rhetorical question, but MJ took me literally. "That kid's got a big mouth. I shut him up."

I set my yogurt cup down on the coffee table. "Lots of people have big mouths, MJ. You can't go around punching them all in the face or dislocating their shoulder."

He smiled wide.

"Oh, no. You don't get to be proud of yourself for this. You're lucky Janelle was able to talk his parents out of filing a police report."

"He hit me first!"

"I know." This wasn't our first conversation about the fight. MJ had insisted it started when the other boy dissed him. MJ responded in kind. Then the other boy pushed him, MJ pushed back and knocked him to the floor. When the other boy got to his feet, he threw the first punch. "But we can't prove it," I told MJ yet again. "What matters is what we can prove."

"And he's white and I'm Black, so the cops are gonna believe him and not me?"

I didn't want to admit it, even though it was probably true, so I replied with a question of my own. "Why won't you tell us what he said to you? Maybe that would help your case." Janelle had asked MJ too, but he wouldn't tell her either. All he'd say was they were both talking smack.

He stared down at the remains of his meatball sub and mumbled, "He called my mom a druggy whore."

I let out a slow breath while I tried to think of an appropriate response. Alex had essentially said the same about Maria. Although he'd said it to me, not to MJ. "Do you miss your mom?"

MJ shrugged. "Sometimes. Do you miss your family?"

I nodded. "All the time."

"I don't miss her all the time, only some of the time. And I only miss the way she used to be before my dad died. But I like living with you and Aunt Maddy."

He and Sofia had both started calling my aunt Aunt Maddy. We never told them to call her that, they just fell into it on their own.

"There's always food in the fridge, and she's got lots of channels on TV," MJ continued.

I laughed. At least, he was clear about his priorities. "Well, I know Aunt Maddy likes having you there."

"Nah, Aunt Maddy just likes Sofia. But that's okay."

He didn't seem upset by this revelation; he recited it as a matter of fact. But I still cried, "That's not true!" Although I wouldn't have wanted to put my hand on a bible and swear to it. Aunt Maddy didn't seem to mind having MJ at her house, but she definitely didn't dote on him the way she doted on Sofia. Not that MJ would've tolerated all that hugging and kissing if she'd tried. Other than that one hug in the school parking lot, he'd never touched me.

MJ might not have been bothered by Aunt Maddy's clear preference for Sofia because it was just as obvious that I preferred his company. The few times Sofia and I were alone together, I'd tried to forge a connection, but she wasn't responsive to me the way she was with my aunt. Maybe she sensed my reticence.

But MJ and Sofia came as a package, we knew that. And my aunt and I were too. So long as the four of us stayed together, the relationship worked. We just had to get the court to agree.

THE NEXT MORNING was more hectic than usual. We were due in family court at ten a.m. for the first custody hearing. I'd purchased khakis and a white button down shirt for MJ, which he'd put on without objection, but Aunt Maddy had bought Sofia a frilly pink monstrosity of a dress, which Sofia refused to wear because it was itchy. It was a rare display of defiance from Sofia, and Aunt Maddy didn't handle it well. I figured Aunt Maddy was just nervous about the custody hearing. I was too.

When the four of us finally managed to leave the house—with Sofia in the purple flowered dress she'd worn the day before that she loved both because it was purple, her favorite color, and not itchy—we sped to the courthouse and ended up only a few minutes late for our pre-hearing meeting with Janelle. She was waiting for us in the hallway outside the courtroom where the hearing would take place.

Neither Aunt Maddy nor I were required to be there. The kids were being represented by Janelle and their social worker. But we both wanted to be there and Janelle said we could come.

Janelle was talking to the kids, telling them what to expect once we went inside the courtroom, when my phone pinged. I read the text message from an unknown number.

It's Alex. Where are you?

Courthouse I texted back. *Kids' first custody hearing.*

Can you postpone?

No. Why?

Found Maria.

Chapter 42

I PULLED Janelle away from the kids and showed her my text exchange with Alex.

"Jesus fucking Christ," she said.

It was the first time I'd heard her curse. "That bad?" I asked.

"What's his number?"

I read off the digits and she punched it into her phone.

"What's wrong?" Aunt Maddy asked, joining us by the window, leaving Sofia sitting on a bench with MJ.

"Alex found Maria," I replied.

"What does that mean?" She looked from me to Janelle, but Janelle walked away from us as she continued her conversation with Alex.

"Nothing good."

JANELLE HUNG up with Alex and called MJ's and Sofia's social worker, who still hadn't arrived at the courthouse, and together they called the judge's clerk and asked for a delay. The judge agreed to postpone the hearing until that afternoon. That gave us a few hours to figure out what to do with this new information. Janelle told us to take the kids back to Aunt Maddy's house while she talked to the social worker. She'd meet up with us later.

"I don't understand any of this," Aunt Maddy said in a low voice. We were huddled together in the kitchen because we didn't want the kids to overhear. Although they knew something was up or, at least, MJ did because he asked me. I told him I wasn't sure what was happening and that Janelle would explain everything when she arrived. I was expecting Alex too. He texted he was driving up from LA. He wanted to talk to MJ in person instead of over the phone.

"We knew this would happen eventually," I said, even though I'd secretly hoped it wouldn't. "No one thought Maria was gone for good. Sooner or later she was going to turn up."

"But she didn't just turn up," Aunt Maddy said. "You went out and found her!"

"Seriously? You're blaming this on me?"

"Well, you're the one who told Alex to hire an investigator."

I understood her being upset. I was upset too. But I couldn't believe she was taking her anger out on me. "If Alex's guy hadn't found her, someone else would've. Once MJ and Sofia entered foster care again, CPS started looking for Maria. They're legally required to."

"Oh, enough with the legal requirements already," she said and started pacing the kitchen. "I don't care about the law."

"Well, I do."

"Then you should be their foster parent, not me. I can't believe I let you drag me into this." She stormed out of the kitchen and a minute later I heard the front door slam shut. I raced out to the living room and watched through the big picture window as her old Subaru peeled out of the driveway and down the street.

MJ jumped up from the couch and joined me. Even Sofia abandoned her dolls and stood next to me.

"Where'd Aunt Maddy go?" Sofia asked.

I looked down at her anxious face and forced a smile. "She just needed a time-out. Don't worry. She'll be back soon." I hoped that was true.

MJ looked wary but returned to his spot on the couch and Sofia curled up next to him. I sat in the side chair pretending to watch *SpongeBob SquarePants* with them, while surreptitiously glancing out the front window every few seconds as if I could will my aunt to return home. When I heard a car approach, I stood up but was disappointed to see Janelle's black sedan pulling into the driveway instead of Aunt Maddy's station wagon.

I opened the front door while Janelle was still walking up. The expression on her face told me she was not bringing good news.

Chapter 43

THE FOUR OF us sat around the dining room table.

"Where's your aunt?" Janelle asked, as if just now noticing she wasn't in the room.

"She's in time-out," Sofia replied.

"Time-out?" Janelle turned to me.

"She needed to clear her head. I'll call and let her know you're here." I grabbed my phone from the table and left the room.

I called Aunt Maddy from the hallway. Her phone rang and rang until eventually her voicemail kicked in. Instead of leaving a message, I texted.

Where are you?

Janelle's here.

You need to come home.

I stared at the three dots, waiting for her response. It took an inordinately long time. Or maybe it just felt that way. Finally, my phone pinged. *Start without me.*

I tried calling her again, and again she didn't pick up. I texted, *Why aren't you answering?*

This time the response came quicker. *On the phone with your mother.*

Hang up with her and call me back.

Can't.

I thought there'd be more, but the three dots disappeared. I returned to the dining room and sat down. "She said to start without her." I said and sat down.

"Is there a problem?" Janelle asked.

"No," I replied.

She stared at me expectantly. When I didn't offer any more information she turned her attention back to the kids. "So, like I was saying, some nice man found your mommy and brought her to the hospital."

"Mommy's sick?" Sofia asked.

"Mommy's always sick," MJ replied and folded his arms across his chest.

"But she'll get better," Janelle said focusing on Sofia. "She's going to meet with a judge soon, just like you. That judge is going to tell her she needs to get better first before she can live with you again."

"You mean he's going to tell her she can go to rehab or jail," MJ said.

It wasn't a question, but Janelle answered anyway. "Yes, and we presume she'll choose rehab."

"She always does," MJ muttered.

"So what does that mean for them?" I asked Janelle.

"It means the kids will stay here with you and your aunt for the time being," Janelle replied. "Reunification is always the goal, but first Maria will have to complete rehab, find a job, a new apartment, and—"

"We have an apartment," MJ said.

Janelle glanced at me before responding to MJ. "Apparently, no one paid the rent this month and the landlord filed for eviction. I'm sorry. I just found out this morning from your social worker." Janelle turned to me. "You should take MJ over there today so he can pick up their stuff before it gets tossed out."

I nodded in response, and Janelle turned back to MJ and Sofia. "Once your mom is better, the judge will let you visit her. Once she can show the judge that she can take care of you, you can live with her again. Is that what you want?"

"Yes!" Sofia said. "I want Mama."

At that moment I was glad Aunt Maddy wasn't in the room. She would've been crushed by Sofia's response.

Janelle turned to MJ. "Is that what you want too?"

"I go where Sofia goes," he said, then turned to me. "Sorry, Grace."

"You don't need to apologize," I said, feeling the tears welling up in my eyes. "You're a good big brother." I reached across the table and squeezed his hand, but I felt him tense and quickly let go.

I was relieved when I heard a knock on the front door. It gave me an excuse to leave the room.

"You okay?" Alex asked when I opened the front door.

I nodded and wiped my eyes and led him to the dining room. As soon as he appeared in the doorway, both kids ran to him. He lifted Sofia up and held her on his hip then did a bro hug with MJ.

"What'd I miss?" he asked.

"Mama's back!" Sofia shouted.

"She is? Where is she? I don't see her. Is she playing hide and seek." Alex pretended to look around the room for her.

Sofia giggled, but MJ rolled his eyes.

"She got picked up," MJ said. "She's going to rehab so she doesn't have to stay in jail."

"Who's going to rehab?" Aunt Maddy asked, joining us. I

hadn't heard her come in. Her eyes were red rimmed, so I knew she'd been crying, but she smiled at the kids and asked, "Who's hungry?"

She pulled a bakery box out from behind her back but decided since it was lunchtime, the kids should eat something substantial first. No one felt like cooking so Alex ordered two pizzas. While we waited for the food to arrive, Janelle repeated to Alex and Aunt Maddy what she'd already told me and the kids.

After Sofia had eaten one slice of pizza and MJ had eaten four and they'd each had a cupcake, Aunt Maddy sent them into the living room so the adults could talk in private. That's when Alex told us that his guy had found Maria unconscious in an abandoned house in Oxnard where lots of junkies liked to crash.

"He called 911 and left," Alex explained. "The paramedics must've brought Maria to the ER and they called the cops."

"You can be arrested for overdosing?" I asked. No one had arrested me when I swallowed half a bottle of sleeping pills.

"Not for overdosing," Janelle said. "But if they think you're selling drugs or you're on probation, then yes, it's pretty common."

"What now?" Aunt Maddy asked.

Janelle paused, then said, "When I asked the kids if they wanted to live with Maria again, they both said yes. I'm sorry, Maddy. I know that's not the answer you were hoping for."

She nodded but didn't reply.

"Let me talk to them," Alex said. "I'll convince them they're better off here with you two."

"Thank you," Aunt Maddy said, at the same time Janelle told Alex "I cannot let you do that."

"You can't let me?" he replied, his voice rising. "I'm not asking."

To her credit, Janelle kept her voice steady. "You cannot

coerce my clients to stay in foster care, Mr. Perez. The State's interest is in reunification, and MJ and Sofia have expressed to me that is their preference as well."

"But they're kids," Aunt Maddy said. "Don't we, as the adults, get to decide what's best for them?"

"Yeah," Alex parroted, "what she said."

Janelle calmly replied, "It's the judge's decision, not ours. The judge will determine what's in their best interests."

"Fuck the judge," Alex said. "He doesn't know those kids."

"Exactly," Aunt Maddy replied. "You should let us talk to the judge. We can tell him what's best."

Janelle took a deep breath before she responded. "Dependency court judges do not generally hear testimony from foster parents or relatives who aren't caregivers. If you want to submit relevant information in writing, I can pass it on. But let's be clear here, I do not represent any of you. My clients are MJ and Sofia, and they've both told me they want to reunite with their mother. That is what I'm going to tell the judge, who's a she, by the way, along with my recommendation that my clients remain in foster care until such time as Maria is able to care for them."

"And how long will that take?" Aunt Maddy asked.

"I don't know," Janelle said. "It could be six months, a year, even longer. It's really up to Maria."

"So I'm just supposed to care for her kids for months or even years, until one day she swoops in and takes them back?" Aunt Maddy said, the tears welling in her eyes.

Janelle's voice softened. "Yes, Maddy. That's how foster care works. I thought you understood that."

Aunt Maddy wiped her eyes with the back of her hands. "You'll have to excuse me," she said, then abruptly left the room. We listened to her footsteps as she ran up the stairs. A moment later we heard a door slam shut.

MJ appeared in the dining room. "Is Aunt Maddy okay?"

All eyes turned to me. "She will be."

"Will she?" Janelle asked.

"Yes," I said and focused on MJ. "Do you want another cupcake?"

"Sure," he said, "if you got some."

"You can have mine," I replied and handed him a napkin and my untouched dessert. "Just keep an eye on Sofia, okay?"

He nodded and headed back to the living room.

"You need to talk to your aunt," Janelle said when it was just the three of us again. "If she doesn't want to foster them anymore, I need to know that before we go back to court this afternoon."

My heart began to race. "You think she doesn't want them here anymore?"

"This is an emergency placement," Janelle said. "If she can't commit to care for them until they can be reunited with their mother, it would be in their best interests to be moved to another foster home that can."

"No," I said. "We're not moving them somewhere else. If Aunt Maddy doesn't want to do this anymore, they can just live with me at my house."

"You're not the foster parent," Janelle said. "You know that. You have no standing here."

"I don't care. They're my kids too. You know I can take care of them."

"What I *know* is irrelevant," Janelle replied. "What matters is the law, and you know that as well as I do."

Yes, in my head I knew what she said was true. But in my heart they were mine. I was sure Aunt Maddy felt the same, at least about Sofia.

Janelle's phone buzzed and she stood up. "I need to go. I've got another hearing at two. Can you bring the kids back to court later?"

I nodded.

"Please talk to your aunt in the meantime. If we need to find a new foster placement, I need to know that before the hearing. I need to let their social worker know too."

I nodded again. "I'll talk to her."

"Good," Janelle said and grabbed another slice of cold pizza on her way out the door.

I dropped my head in my hands and sighed.

"Don't you know, counselor, no good deed goes unpunished."

I turned to Alex, who was already standing up. Then he left too and I was all alone. When I could put off the conversation no longer, I climbed the stairs and knocked on my aunt's bedroom door.

Chapter 44

"Come in," Aunt Maddy said in response to my knock.

She sat up on her bed, her shirt wrinkled, her eyes red rimmed and puffy. "Is it time to leave already?"

"No," I said and sat down on the foot of her bed. "We still have half an hour."

She nodded but didn't say anything.

"You don't have to come to the hearing this afternoon. I can take the kids myself. But I do need to know if you still want to do this."

Her eyes watered. "I'm sorry, Grace, but I don't think I do."

"But why?" I cried, even though I knew the answer. "It could be months or even years before Maria regains custody, assuming she ever does. We don't even know for sure that she wants custody again."

"Of course, she wants custody," Aunt Maddy said. "They're her children. And the longer they stay here, the worse it will be when we have to give them up."

"But it's not a given that she'll be able to get them back. We could fight her. You know Alex is on our side. And MJ only said he wanted to live with her again because Sofia does. I know he'd

208

rather stay with us. Maybe he can convince Sofia. You see the way she follows him around like a puppy."

Aunt Maddy shook her head. "No, Grace. I'm not like you. I don't get energized by the fight. I want peace."

"Please, Aunt Maddy, I'm begging you. Don't do this." The tears were now welling in my eyes too.

"I'm sorry, Grace. I really am. But if we're going to lose them, I think it would be better if it happened sooner rather than later. I'm just not cut out for this."

AUNT MADDY WAS the one who called Janelle and told her. And I was the one who splashed cold water on my face, donned my sunglasses, and drove MJ and Sofia to the courthouse alone.

Janelle told me I didn't need to come inside the courtroom, that I could just wait on the bench outside, but I insisted. I also insisted I be the one to tell MJ he and Sofia would be moving to another foster home. He acted like it was no big deal, but I still felt awful. And despite him pretending otherwise, I think he was upset too. When I hugged him, he didn't pull away.

When the judge called their case, I sat at the front table with MJ, Sofia, Janelle, the social worker, and an attorney for the County.

The judge looked down the row at each of us, then back down to her file.

"Is there a parent here?" she asked.

"No, your honor," the county attorney responded. "Father's deceased. The mother's in custody. But we expect her to go to rehab in lieu of jail time."

The judge nodded. "So the plan is reunification?"

"Yes," the social worker replied.

The judge asked MJ and Sofia if they wanted to live with their mother again, and they both said yes.

"Are we keeping the current foster placement?" the judge asked.

"No, your honor," the social worker answered. "The current placement is temporary. I'm arranging for a longer-term placement."

"Very well," the judge said. "Notify the court of the new placement, and we'll meet again in six months." She rapped her gavel and we all stood.

"That's it?" I whispered to Janelle as we filed out of the courtroom.

"That's it," she replied.

The hearing hadn't even lasted five minutes.

Once we were outside the courtroom, the social worker asked if my aunt could keep the kids overnight. She was already in touch with another foster family, but they were fostering other children too and wanted a night to prepare.

"Of course," I said. "We can keep them as long as you need."

"Thanks. I'll text you with a pickup time."

I drove the kids back to my aunt's house and filled her in. She didn't look any happier about this than I was. "It's not too late to change your mind," I said, although I wasn't sure that was true.

"It's for the best," Aunt Maddy replied.

I disagreed, but didn't say so. "I need to take MJ back to their apartment so he can pack up the rest of their things."

"Do you want me to hold dinner for you?" she asked.

"No. We'll grab something while we're out. You're okay watching Sofia tonight?"

"Of course," Aunt Maddy replied.

NEITHER MJ nor I spoke while we drove to his apartment. We found the eviction notice taped to the front door. This was the third day of the three-day notice, so it was good that we arrived tonight. By tomorrow their belongings might've already been dumped in the trash.

I flipped the light switch and was happy to find that the power was still on. I was sure there were past-due notices from the utility company in the overstuffed mailbox, but there was no point in getting them. No one was going to pay.

I'd grabbed a handful of lawn and leaf bags from Aunt Maddy's house before we left, but we only needed two. MJ didn't want any of his or Sofia's clothes. He said the new clothes Aunt Maddy and I had bought them were nicer. But he stuffed some of Maria's clothes into one of the bags along with a small wooden box. The other bag he used for their photo albums.

I wanted to leave right away, but MJ wanted to show me pictures of his family first, so we sat down on the filthy couch and looked through the photo albums together. I saw images of MJ's dad, both formal shots of him in uniform and family photos of a much younger MJ and his father playing football together, eating ice cream cones (with MJ's dripping all over his shirt), and showing off their respective muscles at the beach. I laughed at the baby pictures of MJ, his face covered in whatever his parents had been trying to feed him, sometimes with an empty bowl overturned on his head. Occasionally, Maria was in these photos too, although it seemed more often she was the one behind the camera.

There were lots of photos of MJ as a baby and a toddler and maybe a dozen of him as a little boy. Not many once MJ turned school age and almost none of Sofia. I knew that wasn't unusual. My Before friends guiltily admitted that while they had hundreds of baby pictures of their first child, they had few of their second. Alex appeared in some of the photos too. He looked exactly the same down to the all-black clothing and the tattoos.

The most shocking images were of Maria. She'd given birth to MJ when she was seventeen and she looked like a child herself. Back then, she had Sofia's lovely caramel complexion, long, shiny black hair, and a figure that straddled the line between curvy and plump.

Her appearance changed dramatically in later photos, which I presumed were taken after MJ's father died and she'd started using drugs. Except for one picture of her with MJ and a very young Sofia standing in front of a Christmas tree, all three smiling with Santa hats on their heads, Maria looked like an entirely different person. Her skin was sallow and marked, her hair was stringy, and her voluptuous curves were gone. Her clothes hung on her like mine hung on me.

I was torn between two emotions—my anger at her for abandoning her children, and my empathy for how she must've felt when her husband died and her whole world fell apart.

I couldn't help but wonder what would've happened to me if only Jonah had died and Amelia had lived? Would I have struggled like Maria? Would I have fallen so far that I would've abandoned my child? I wanted to think not, but no one really knows what they would do until they're in the situation themselves. It's easy to judge when you've never had to walk in the other person's shoes.

After we finished looking through the photo albums, we brought the two trash bags down to my car and drove to Target where I bought two suitcases. I didn't want MJ and Sofia to go to their new home with all their belongings stuffed into garbage bags. I asked MJ what he wanted for dinner, and he chose In-N-Out.

Over burgers and french fries, I apologized again for giving him up. It wasn't my decision, but that fact did not absolve me of my guilt.

He shrugged in response.

"You know if they would let me keep you and Sofia myself I would. They won't."

"Why not?" he asked. "Is it because you got no husband?"

"No, that doesn't matter, at least not in California."

"Then why?"

MJ knew about Jonah and Amelia, but he didn't know about my suicide attempt. I didn't particularly want to tell him now, but I felt like I owed him an honest answer. "I had a hard time after my family died. I didn't do so well."

"Like my mom?" he said.

"Similar."

"Except you're not a junkie," he said, his voiced laced with anger.

"You can't compare our situations, MJ. I had a lot of support, both from my family and financially. Your mom didn't have any of that."

MJ shrugged and stuffed a handful of french fries into his mouth.

I took a deep breath and said, "Despite all that, I still took a bunch of pills and tried to kill myself."

His eyes popped and his forehead wrinkled. "For real?"

"Yes. I had a bad day and did something really stupid."

He smiled. "Like when I dislocated that kid's shoulder?"

I laughed. "Yes. And please promise me you're not going to do anything like that again. The last thing you need is to be expelled from school."

"If you promise not to take any more pills."

"Promise," I said, and we shook on it. "So in answer to your question, that's why CPS won't let me be your foster parent. I'm not considered stable."

"But you're better now, right?"

"Better than I was, yes, but I still see a therapist. Have you ever been to therapy? Other than that one time with the school counselor, I mean."

He shook his head, his mouth filled with french fries.

"Would you like to see one? I can arrange it if you want." I didn't see any reason why his new foster family would object if I was willing to pay.

He washed down his french fries with a long sip of Coke. "What do you do in therapy?"

"Talk mostly."

"About what?"

"Whatever's on your mind. A lot about feelings. Therapists really like to talk about how you feel."

"Sounds boring," he said and took another bite of his burger.

"Not really. And it can help, with the anger and the other stuff."

He didn't answer me. He just kept eating.

Finally I said, "You don't need to decide tonight. You can think about it and let me know."

"How?" he asked.

"How what?"

"How am I gonna let you know? I ain't never gonna see you again."

Chapter 45

"THAT'S NOT TRUE!" I cried as my stomach seized. "Of course, we'll still see each other." MJ was a part of my life now. Sofia was too, even if spending time with her made me sad. I couldn't fathom never seeing them again.

MJ pushed his red plastic tray away from him, even though it still contained a few french fries, and folded his arms across his chest. "No, we won't. I ain't never seen any of my other foster parents."

"Well, I can't speak for your other foster parents, I can only speak for myself. You will definitely see me again."

He pushed the tray even further towards my side of the table and snorted. "Yeah, right."

I pushed the tray back towards him. It had somehow become a proxy for our relationship. "Yes, right. Even if we don't live together, we can still be friends, can't we? Plus, I'm your boss. You think I'm going to keep paying you if you don't show up for work?"

"You still want me to work for you?"

"I have to. You're the only one who knows how to fix the printer when it jams."

. . .

THE SOCIAL WORKER insisted on picking up MJ and Sofia the next morning, even though I told her MJ had already missed too much school and she should pick him up in the afternoon instead. Aunt Maddy had packed up Sofia's clothes and toys the night before. Early the next morning, she hugged them both goodbye and left the house. She said she didn't want to be there when the social worker took them away. I didn't agree with her decision, but I understood.

When the social worker arrived and saw how much luggage they had—one large suitcase and a backpack for MJ, a smaller suitcase for Sofia, and several shopping bags filled with toys—she balked.

"Kids have one bag at most," she said.

"Is there some sort of cap on luggage in the Child Welfare Code? Do you charge extra for bags now like the airlines?"

"No."

"Then they're legally entitled to bring their stuff with them. Or do I need to get Janelle on the phone?" I added, pulling my cell phone out of my back pocket.

The social worker gave me a petulant look but said, "They can take whatever fits in my car."

We loaded the two suitcases and one of the toy bags into her trunk, and the other two bags we stuffed onto the floor of the backseat. There was no room for Sofia's dollhouse and books. I'd have to deliver them to the new foster home myself.

I strapped Sofia into the booster seat and hugged her good-bye. I walked around to the other side of the car to say goodbye to MJ. "You don't have to come to work today," I said, blinking back tears. "But I expect to see you at the office tomorrow after school. Got it?"

He nodded and stared down at his shoes.

I stood in the driveway and waved to them as the social worker drove them away. After her car turned the corner at the end of the street, I went back inside my aunt's house. I climbed the stairs, laid down on top of my bed, and cried myself back asleep.

MY EYES WERE SWOLLEN when I arrived at Dr. Rubenstein's office. She didn't need to prod the information out of me. As soon as we'd both sat down, I told her everything.

"I'm so sorry, Grace."

I sniffed loudly and wiped away my tears. "It's not as if I wasn't warned. By everyone. This time I have no one to blame but myself."

"That doesn't make it any easier though, does it?"

"No," I agreed. "It doesn't."

It wasn't as painful as losing Jonah and Amelia. MJ and Sofia weren't dead. I would see them again. But my chest still ached, and every time I thought about them in the backseat of the social worker's car driving away from me, I started to cry. It was as if the two losses had somehow fused together into one giant heartache.

"What are you going to do now?" Dr. Rubenstein asked.

I shrugged. "I'm open to suggestions."

She re-crossed her legs and shifted in her seat. "I have one for you, but you're not going to like it."

I smiled through my tears. "I'm already miserable, so you might as well tell me."

"I think now would be a good time for you to pack up Jonah's and Amelia's things."

I laughed. "Really? You want me to compound my misery?"

She leaned forward in her seat. "I'm not suggesting it will give you closure, because that's not possible. You will carry their deaths with you always. But wounds do heal in time, if you let them. First, though, you need to let yourself grieve."

"You don't think I've grieved? How can you say that to me? I've done nothing but grieve for the last year and a half."

"In your head, yes, but not here," she said, placing her hands on her chest. "Not in your heart. You will do anything to avoid feeling the pain. And that's natural. But there are no shortcuts, Grace. The only way out of the pain is through it."

I leaned my head back and closed my eyes. "I can't believe you think today is the day to do this."

"I do. You've been putting it off a long time, Grace. Too long. Make today the day you let yourself truly grieve for them and say goodbye. Only then can you start to heal."

There was nothing in the world I wanted to do less than what she was suggesting. But I couldn't go on this way. Even I knew that. Something had to change. I had to find a way out. I didn't know if she was right, but at this point, I was willing to try anything.

Chapter 46

I DROVE DIRECTLY from Dr. Rubenstein's office to my house in The Hills. Today the driveway was empty and the front door was locked. I dropped the mail and my purse on the kitchen counter and headed straight to the garage, which still contained the empty boxes Jonah used to save from our online deliveries. I used to tease him about it. I argued we'd never use them again and they just ate up space in the garage. But today they would get a second life.

I dusted off an armload of boxes and carried them upstairs. I stopped at the second floor landing and turned my head towards Amelia's room, like I always did. But instead of heading in the other direction, today I stepped inside.

Everything looked exactly the same as when Amelia was alive but for a layer of dust. The white dresser stood under the window with the moon and stars nightlight in one corner and a stack of children's books in the other. The changing table with the fuzzy pink pad was just inside the bedroom door and the rocking chair on its other side. On the opposite wall was the white crib with the pink swan sheets I spent hours obsessing over online. All that was missing was the baby. She wasn't there now and she never would be again.

All that useless worrying—cloth diapers or disposable, breast milk or formula, organic or non-organic—it never occurred to me to worry about a madman with a gun. If I had worried about that instead would Amelia be alive today? If I had kept her home with me that morning instead of sending her to the bakery with Jonah, she would be. My daughter died because of my selfish need for a few minutes of alone time.

"No," I said aloud to the empty room. "You do not get to blame yourself for this." I didn't think this was what Dr. Ruben-stein had in mind when she said I needed to let myself feel the pain. Intellectually I knew I was not responsible for Amelia's death, but in my heart...

Stop it, Grace, just stop it.

I snatched up the empty boxes and hurried out of the room, slamming the door shut behind me, as if my own thoughts wouldn't follow me wherever I went. I'd start with Jonah's things. Even I couldn't find a way to blame myself for his death. It had been his idea to walk down to the bakery for croissants that morning, not mine. I'd told him I was fine with cereal.

Two HOURS and five boxes later Jonah's clothes and shoes were packed away. I kept his wedding ring, the watch I'd bought him for his thirtieth birthday, and the cashmere sweater I loved. The rest would find a new home with a local charity.

I only had one empty box left, but it was large and Amelia's clothes were small.

You are not responsible for her death. They were both in the wrong place at the wrong time. This was not your fault.

I repeated the words over and over in my head until I'd

convinced myself they were true. Then I opened her bedroom door and walked inside.

Chapter 47

I HEADED STRAIGHT to the dresser with my head down. I pulled open the top drawer and immediately spotted the pink and blue beanie the hospital gave to all the newborn babies, and I started to cry. But I didn't stop. I let my tears fall as I pulled out each onesie, each pair of socks, each adorable outfit that my mother or my aunt or a friend had given us as a baby gift. I inhaled each item's nonexistent scent, refolded it, and placed it inside the box.

I set aside the beanie, my favorite pink onesie with the words *princess in training* embroidered across the front, and a sunny yellow sweater my mother had knitted for Amelia that was two sizes too big and she never had the opportunity to grow into. The rest of the clothes I packed away. When I'd finished, there was still a few inches of empty space in the box.

My gaze landed on the stack of books: *Goodnight Moon*, *Madeline*, and a boxed set of Sandra Boynton board books I received from one of my former co-workers as a shower gift. I could probably fit them in the box with the clothes if I tried.

No, not the books. I'd read to Amelia every night from the day we'd brought her home from the hospital until the night before she died. Even though none of the stories had ever put her to sleep like they were supposed to, I still treasured that time together. Amelia had stared up at me so intently, it was as if she'd actually understood the words I'd read to her. I allowed myself to wallow in the memory and the tears came harder.

No spiraling, I admonished. I laid the beanie, the onesie, and the sweater on top of the dresser next to the books. I'd go out later and buy one of those watertight containers to store them in. That way, no matter what happened, I'd know these small pieces I had left would always be safe.

I folded the flaps of the box closed and sat down in the rocking chair. My mother had been trying to convince me to donate Amelia's furniture since the day after the funeral. I knew she was right, just as everyone had been right about MJ and Sofia. But I couldn't just throw a crib and a dresser in the back of my small SUV. The furniture would have to wait for another day.

"Okay," I said to the empty room, "You got me here. Now what?"

The room didn't answer, not that I expected it to.

I glanced at the changing table with its still-full diaper caddy attached to the side and smiled. The diaper caddy was full because Jonah refilled it every night before he went to bed. He told me it was because he didn't want me to run out of diapers when he wasn't home. He knew it was difficult for me to pull down the giant box of diapers that resided on the top shelf of the closet, especially if I was also holding a squirming baby too.

Thank you, Jonah. You were a thoughtful husband and a wonderful father. I miss you so much, sometimes my heart literally aches for you. And I miss you too, darling Amelia. I hope wherever you and Daddy are now, you're having lots of father-daughter bonding time. I'm so sorry you never got the chance to grow up. Maybe wherever you are that doesn't matter. Or maybe wherever you are now, you will get to grow up and live the life there that you never got to live here. I hope so. Please know that you were loved so much and that you always will be. I will never stop loving you. Never.

I laid down on the floor in a ball and cried and cried until I had no tears left.

I HEARD the front door open and slam shut, then feet pounding on the stairs. By the time my aunt appeared in the doorway to Amelia's bedroom, I was sitting upright.

"Thank God!" she cried and dropped down to her knees beside me before pulling me into a fierce hug.

"What's wrong?" I asked. "What happened?"

She stopped hugging me and held me at arm's length. "What's wrong? What's wrong is you don't answer your goddamn phone!" She pulled her own phone out of her purse and called my mother. "She's fine," Aunt Maddy said. I could only hear my aunt's side of the conversation but she was nodding her head saying, "yes, yes, I will, don't worry." She held the phone out to me. "Your mother wants to speak to you."

"Hello."

"You scared us half to death," my mother yelled. "What were you thinking?"

"What did I do?"

"I called. Your aunt called. She even texted. We had no idea what happened to you."

"What did you think happened?"

"We didn't know," she yelled. "That's the point. After they took the kids away, well, we didn't know what you'd do."

I closed my eyes and sighed. Now I understood. "You thought I tried to kill myself again."

"You were upset. We didn't know what you'd do. But when we couldn't reach you —"

"You assumed the worst."

My mother's voice softened. "We were scared, sweetheart. Don't be angry. We just wanted to know you were okay."

"I'm okay, Mom." I said it reflexively, but then I thought about it and realized it was actually true. I wasn't happy. Definitely, not happy. But it was as if a weight had been lifted somehow. I felt like I could finally breathe again.

I handed the phone back to my aunt, and she told my mother she'd call her later and hung up. I went to the bathroom and splashed cold water on my face. When I returned to Amelia's bedroom, my aunt had opened the box and was peering inside.

"You packed up Amelia's clothes," she said.

I nodded. "It was time."

She reached for my hand and squeezed. "I'm so proud of you."

I actually laughed. "Proud of me? For what? For finally doing the one thing you all begged me to do ages ago?"

"You did it now and that's all that matters. Do you need help carrying it down to the car?"

"Yeah, that'd be great."

Aunt Maddy nodded at the changing table. "Do you want to donate the furniture too?"

"Yes, but I need to call first and see what they take and if they'll come pick it up. But I should drop off the diapers. The children's charities are always asking for diapers. There's a box at the top of the closet. I'll go get the stepstool."

I ran downstairs and stopped in the kitchen on my way to the laundry room, which is where the stepstool lived. I pulled my phone out of my purse and saw all the missed calls from my mother and my aunt, along with two text messages. One was from my aunt. The other was from MJ. *New place OK. CU tomorrow.*

I closed my eyes and whispered, "Thank God."

I grabbed the stepstool and carried it upstairs to Amelia's room. I found Aunt Maddy standing next to a pile of diapers, which she must've pulled out of the diaper caddy since it was now lying empty on the floor.

"One question," she said, and held up her hand. Standing upright between her thumb and forefinger was a small black rectangular piece of plastic. "Why do you keep a flash drive inside your diaper caddy?"

"I don't. It must've fallen in there when Jonah was filling it."

"I doubt that," she said. "I found it taped to the bottom."

The images rushed at me like a series of flashbacks in a movie. The day I found the second life insurance policy in the safe deposit box; my mother telling me to stop looking for trouble where none existed; the time I came home and found Jake at my house; him pulling his key out of his pocket and telling me Jonah had given it to him; and me sitting in Jonah's still-warm chair realizing Jake had been sitting in it before me. Jake had been searching for something that day.

I stared at the flash drive in my aunt's hand.

Is this what Jake had been looking for?

Oh my God, Jonah. What did you do?

A Note from the Author

Thank you for reading *Fall from Grace*. I sincerely hope you enjoyed it. Book 2 in the series, *The Lies We Tell*, will be released on August 1, 2023. Book 3 in the series, *The Truth of It*, will be released on August 22, 2023.

If you enjoyed this book, please consider leaving a review. While word of mouth is still the best way to discover new books in my opinion, those online reviews help too! If you could spend a few minutes leaving a review at Goodreads or your preferred online retailer I would be extremely grateful.

Thank you!

About the Author

Beth Orsoff is an Amazon bestseller and the author of twelve novels ranging from romantic comedies to domestic suspense. You can find information about all of Beth's books and contact her at www.bethorsoff.com. While you're there you can sign up for her mailing list and she'll send you a free ebook!

Made in the USA
Las Vegas, NV
13 November 2023

80787617R00142